The Stand at Paxton County

Story

Carl Morris

Screenplay by

David M. O'Neill

EXT. HOAG RAFFERTY FIELD - 7 AM - DAY

Paxton County North Dakota.

Frozen, stark landscapes lift and blend, greeting the morning
horizon - yet, another unforgiving Dakota, Sioux Nation
winter.

Grazing fences down, barn boards dilapidated, tractors frozen
in their fields.

Thin horses scatter about - frigid, equine snouts scratch the
arctic-like earth for sparse reeds of grass.

Lifetime Paxton County ranchers DELL CONNELLY (60) and TOM
GARDNER (60's) vigorously lower bale's of hay from the back
of Tom's old Ford flatbed.

                    DELL
          Those horses are listless. Cracked
          hooves. Over there, that dun mare's
          missing a lot of hair.

                    TOM
          More than normal. I'm counting ribs
          on at least half of them.

Sheriff's patrol car sits empty near the distant farmhouse.

                    DELL
          Hoag wouldn't last fifteen minutes
          out here making repairs on his own.
          Sheriff knows that.

                    TOM
          Been in there forty-minutes now.

EXT. HOAG RAFFERTY FARM HOUSE - EARLY MORNING - DAY

Two men emerge and make for the barn.

A hallowed-out old man, HOAG RAFFERTY (80'S), and a muscular,
taught-looking, SHERIFF ROGER STEINER (60).

The sheriff - all business. Old Hoag Rafferty, the blunt-end
of it.

                    TOM
          That doesn't look good.

INT. 1997 CHEVY SUV - 7:30 AM - DAY

JOSH FALVEY (40'S), Fergus Falls Dailey lone field-reporter
ambles up the rural road in his outdated, dirty SUV.

Josh sips his coffee. KWGO Minot Radio spills with weather reports and news.

> RADIO (V.O.)
> Storms across the Great Plains yesterday, a handful of tornadoes touched down across the region. No reports of property damage or injuries...

Passenger seat - loose pens, notes. Yellow pad note reads: *"Animal Abuse - Anonymous"*.

Right-front-tire smacks a deep road rut - morning brew plows down Josh's chin and lap like a hot, staining waterfall.

> JOSH
> Ow. Ow, ow... Sone-of-a...

EXT. HOAG RAFFERTY FIELD GATE - 7:35 - DAY

Josh's SUV comes a stop near Dell and Tom.

He gets out of his vehicle - approaches Dell and Tom with a coffee-stained shirt and crotch.

> JOSH
> Morning, boys. Josh Falvey from the Fergus Falls Daily.

> TOM
> Looks like some coffee had you for breakfast.

Josh inventories his newly acquired shirt stains.

> JOSH
> More like a rut down there had me for lunch.

> DELL
> What brings you out here this early?

> JOSH
> Sunday piece to come out in a couple of weeks - how ranchers have fared through the winter.

Josh steps up and looks out toward the field - takes a few pictures.

> JOSH (CONT'D)
> (beat)
> Those Hoag's horses out there?

> DELL
> Yep. 2's and 3's, no 4's and 6's.
> But we'll get 'em there. He's in
> the barn with the Sheriff going
> over compliance issues. You should
> write about that in your Sunday
> piece.

Josh turns and walks to the barn.

> JOSH
> Will keep it in mind. Thanks.

INT. RAFFERTY BARN - EARLY MORNING - DAY

Old Man Rafferty pleads his case with the Sheriff.

> HOAG RAFFERTY
> Winter's been hard on all of us,
> Roger.

> SHERIF BOSTWICK
> I understand that, Hoag. Everybody
> does.(beat) But, maybe there's a
> way out of all of this.

EXT. HOAG RAFFERTY BARN - EARLY MORNING - DAY

Josh, circles the Sheriff's patrol vehicle and walks toward
the opening of the barn door.

Josh goes inside the barn.

EXT. HOAG RAFFERTY FIELD - MORNING - DAY

Dell's hand reaches out gently for the back of the Dun Mare's
neck.

> DELL (O.S.)
> That's it. Easy. Easy. I know -
> been a long winter hasn't it, old
> girl?

He gives a passing look back to the barn.

Dell's eyes twitch from an unusual, light, sting of pain -
open palm-feeds the horse some morning grains.

                         DELL (CONT'D)
              We'll get you some meat on those
              bones.

A noxious sweat begins to bead from Dell's brow - he rubs his
forehead - begins to grow disoriented.

                         DELL (CONT'D)
                    (breathless)
              Tom...

Suddenly, a shot **explodes** from inside the barn! Blood and
glass blow through a side-barn window.

Tom quickly turns.

Dell collapses in the field of frozen mud - falling beneath
the dangerous weight of the dun mare above.

Tom rushes towards his friend.

                         TOM
              Dell!!

EXT. HOAG RAFFERTY BARN - MORNING - DAY

Sheriff Bostwick steps out filling the barn doorway. Patrol
vehicle - he reaches inside for his dash radio.

                         SHERIFF BOSTWICK
                    (calm)
              Annie, it's Roger. We have two men
              down out at the Rafferty ranch.
              Rocky Run Creek out near South
              Cottonwood. Possible heart attack,
              need an ambulance. Second man down,
              fatal gunshot wound, possible
              accident, probable suicide. Medics
              and forensics - thanks, Annie.

INT. AFGHANISTAN, U.S. TRIAGE MEDICAL TENT - DAY

Forward front-line position medic, U.S. CAPTAIN JANNA
CONNELLY (26), along with U.S. ARMY MAJOR KAREEM R.
KHAN(40's) slam open the rectangular medical field tent
carrying a severely wounded, U.S. ARMY FIRST CLASS CORPORAL
RIOS (25).

                     SCREEN READS
        41ST BRIGADE INFANTRY MEDICAL - HERAT PROVINCE

Janna pulls back the corporal's pant-leg. From the knee down,
it hangs on by less than a thread - blood, and lot's of it.

                         JANNA
          Tourniquet. Get this thing clamped
          off! Major, help me get his shirt
          off.

Major Khan works to the directions of the young Captain.

                         JANNA (CONT'D)
          Thoracic, abdominal, and pelvic
          bleeding.

Massive blood loss.

                         JANNA (CONT'D)
          Exsanguinating hemorrhaging. Prep
          transfusion. Get me 10 units of
          RBC's.

Major Khan looks over his friend.

                         MAJOR KHAN
          God-dammit, Rios...

                         JANNA
          You know this soldier?

                         MAJOR KHAN
          He's in my company, Bravo Command.
          Traded up to point. We got hit,
          bad.

Janna continues examining the soldier's wounds.

                         JANNA
          Multiple fractures, punctures in
          hips, back and head, POSSIBLE
          collapsed left lung, shrapnel back
          of legs, broken right leg.

Two TRIAGE ORDERLIES (30'S) move quickly to assist. They
begin to cut away the rest of the soldier's clothes to access
the wounds.

                         JANNA (CONT'D)
          What happened?

                         MAJOR KHAN
          We were on patrol. Open terrain.
          They came in from the trees from
          the west at about 60 yards. He ran
          up to a forward position, hit an
          IED then we were ambushed.

Corporal Rios momentarily comes back to consciousness.

                    CORPORAL RIOS
          Hey, K. Looks like we got hit
          pretty good, huh?

The Major reaches for his friend's hand.

                    MAJOR KHAN
          You're in good hands now, buddy.
          Just relax and let 'em do their
          thing.

                    JANNA
          Rios? You didn't have to go through
          all this just to get my number, you
          know? You just could've asked.

                    CORPORAL RIOS
               (smiles weakly)
          Just thought doing it this way, be
          a little more dramatic. You
          couldn't refuse me.

                    JANNA
          And, I thought I was a drama queen.

Janna reaches beneath his back and is within whisper-shot
away from the dieing Corporal Rios.

Rios' eyes slightly open.

                    CORPORAL RIOS
               (whisper - breathless)
          Don't let me die here, please. I
          don't want to die. Major K?

Janna shares a close look to the Major. She reaches for the
Corporal's other hand - close up, face to face.

                    MAJOR KHAN
          Please, don't lose him.

Major Khan steps back - frightened, helpless.

                    JANNA
               (whisper - smiles)
          Where are you going to take me?
          Dinner, movie?

INT. U.S. QUONSET HUT SLEEPING QUARTERS - NIGHT

Janna - sound asleep. Blood on her face and field operation
gear lies about - straight 36 hour shift.

Her long-range phone blares near her ear. Startled, she fumbles out the phone, drops it and grabs it again.

                    JANNA
              (catatonic)
          If this is a wrong number, I'm
          gonna' hunt you down.

INT. MARLA'S VETERINARY CLINIC - PAXTON ND - DAY

MARLA ORTON (27), life-long friend of Janna, with phone in ear, puts on white surgical gear heading into an operating room of her own.

                    MARLA
          I take it your still 6,719 miles
          away from me?

                    JANNA (PHONE V.O.)
              (groggy)
          And, counting. Actually, I'm
          hanging at the beach, sipping a
          daiquiri, looking at the boys
          surfing with my toes in the sand.
              (beat) Just off a double-double.
          I'm going to have varicose veins
          before I'm thirty.

                    MARLA
          Listen, your dad is fine, but he
          collapsed yesterday.

INT. U.S. QUONSET HUT SLEEPING QUARTERS - NIGHT

Janna's head snaps-up, eyes open.

                    JANNA
          What? What happened?

                    MARLA (PHONE V.O.)
          He had a heart attack. I was
          reminded I'm not family. They
          didn't tell me squat. I tried. Now,
          if he was a cow I could diagnose
          him.

                    JANNA
          They release him?

                    MARLA (PHONE V.O.)
          In a few days. You better talk to
          your C.O. and get home.

                    JANNA
          How's the place look?

                    MARLA (PHONE V.O.)
          Like you need to get back and take
          out the garbage.

                                        FADE OUT:

                                        FADE IN:

EXT. PAXTON COUNTY - RURAL TWO LANE HIGHWAY - DAY

Janna drives a small rented compact. Rural roads, open
fields, wide open skies, rivers and crumbling, abandoned barn
houses.

Sign reads: Welcome to Paxton County.

INT/EXT. JANNA'S CAR / FOOD MART/GAS STATION - DUSK

Entering the town of Paxton, Janna drives slowly through the
main drag - familiar buildings, old haunts - not much has
changed.

Radio - local music and news.

                    RADIO (V.O.)
          Paxton, Pride of North Dakota,
          spring concert and BBQ, Kurt
          Mandel, headlining straight from
          Dickinson, White Fish's own, Amy
          Grassfield!

Janna turns off the radio.

She pulls into local food mart/gas station. She gets out of
her car - puts on a baseball hat.

INT. FOOD MART/GAS STATION - DUSK

Janna purchases a few dinner items. A LAKOTA INDIAN WOMAN -
(45), bags the groceries, hands back change.

                    LAKOTA ATTENDANT
          My last single. You got lucky.

                    JANNA
          Thanks. You have a bathroom key?

                    LAKOTA ATTENDANT
          Right here. Outside to the left.
          Next!

EXT. STORE PARKING SPACE NEAR BATHROOM - DUSK

10   Near car. Janna opens up the trunk and places her bag of   10
        groceries inside. Heads to the side bathroom door.

INT. FOOD MART/GAS STATION - DUSK

A Paxton County DEPUTY SHERIFF, CARL HAGGEN (27) shops down
the aisle with his back facing the front of the store.

INT. FOOD MART/GAS STATION BATHROOM - DUSK

Janna turns on the faucet, water streams. She takes off her
hat and places it on the sink.

She lets the cool water run over her hands and fingers -
splashes it.

She looks in the mirror - exhausted.

                    JANNA
               (sotto)
          7,000 miles does not wear well on a
          girl. (yawns).

She turns and flips up the toilet seat.

INT. FOOD MART/GAS STATION - DUSK

Two more attractive WOMEN (30's) come in from the outside -
they make their way into the store and break for a respective
aisle.

Deputy Carl finally approaches the station-attendant at the
register.

He places his trail-mix and energy drink down on the counter.

                    LAKOTA ATTENDANT
          You find everything okay?

                    DEPUTY HAGGEN
          I guess this should do it.

The attendant begins to punch in numbers on his cash
register.

                    LAKOTA ATTENDANT
          That'll be 5.50.

The Deputy places down a ten dollar bill.

                    LAKOTA ATTENDANT (CONT'D)
          Ah...

                    DEPUTY HAGGEN
            What is it?

The attendant opens up her cash box.

                    LAKOTA ATTENDANT
            I just gave out my last single.

One women who had entered the store, now stands waiting
behind Deputy Carl.

                    LAKOTA ATTENDANT (CONT'D)
            Do you have another one dollar bill
            by any chance?

                    DEPUTY HAGGEN
            You want me to give you a one and a
            ten? I have five dollars and fifty
            cents worth of stuff.

                    LAKOTA ATTENDANT
            If you give me another one, I can
            give you a five and two quarters
            back. I'm just out of singles
            otherwise I'll have to give you,
            eighteen quarters.

Impatient Woman, rolls her eyes.

                    DEPUTY HAGGEN
            A five and two quarters back?

Janna reenters with the bathroom key in hand. Comes into the
middle of an escalating situation.

                    DEPUTY HAGGEN (CONT'D)
                (beat - anger rising)
            So, let me get this straight. You
            want me to give you a ten dollar
            bill, for five dollars and fifty
            worth of stuff? Then you want me to
            give you another one dollar bill,
            making that eleven-dollars for an
            energy drink and some trail mix.

The attendant senses trouble - remains still.

                    DEPUTY HAGGEN (CONT'D)
            You playing me?

Janna looks up to the back of the Deputy and to the Lakota
woman - keeps alert.

Carl turns back to see the attractive women looking point blank straight at him.

Janna then begins to recognize Carl. His humiliation grows into a steady stream of frustration.

                    STATION ATTENDANT
                   (a bit intimidated)
          Listen, no worries. I'll just...

                    JANNA (O.S.)
          Excuse me, officer? Are you Carl
          Haggen by any chance?

Carl turns back to see Janna stepping up towards him.

                    DEPUTY HAGGEN
          What's that?

                    JANNA
          Yeah. I knew you as PK - the
          Preacher's Kid. Never pictured you
          in law-enforcement, or growing up
          to be a Sheriff?

All eyes on what Janna may be up to.

                    DEPUTY HAGGEN
          I'm Deputy Carl Haggen. We know
          each other?

Janna takes off her hat.

                    JANNA
          I'm Janna Connelly. Remember? We
          went to high school together.

                    DEPUTY HAGGEN
          Holy, shit. Janna Banana!

Carl, distracted from the confusion, turns on a dime. He steps out of line, leaving his items on the counter.

The attendant waves up the others to the front.

                    STATION ATTENDANT
          Who's next?

Janna leads Carl away from the attendant - heading-off possible further trouble.

                    JANNA
          You remember me don't you?

Exiting out the doors with Carl. Janna waves to the attendant behind her back - moving Mr. Muscle out of the store.

> DEPUTY HAGGEN
> Yeah, sure I do. You were working
> in those nursing homes after
> school, or something like that,
> right?

> JANNA
> Good memory, Carl. Yeah...

EXT. FOOD MART/GAS STATION - DUSK

Janna and Carl now stand like old high-school friends catching up.

> DEPUTY HAGGEN
> I think that Lakota woman was
> trying to get one over on me.
> They're always pulling something
> one way of another.

> JANNA
> Just a little confusion. So, Paxton
> County Sheriff, huh?

> DEPUTY HAGGEN
> (a little smitten)
> Well, Deputy. I've got some time
> before I can run for Sheriff.

> JANNA
> Okay. Well, I'm just getting into
> town, so heading up to the ranch,
> but great running in to you, Deputy
> Carl.

> DEPUTY HAGGEN
> Yeah, okay. I'll see you around,
> banana.

Janna turns, spins, gets in her car and goes - escalating scene inside the gas station - all avoided.

Carl walks to his patrol car and gets in.

INT. DEPUTY CARL'S PATROL CAR - DUSK

A bit taken by Janna, Carl puts his key in the ignition.

He then reaches for the snacks he thought he bought. Nowhere to be found.

                         DEPUTY HAGGEN
                       Where's my..?

EXT. CONNELLY RANCH YARD - NIGHT

Janna's car makes its way up the Connelly road - main house,
barn, feed lot in the distance.

EXT. CONNELLY RANCH, FRONT ROOM - NIGHT

She gets out of the car.

Takes an inventory of her old home - lot's of needed work -
more memories, good and bad.

                         JANNA
                  Oh, Dell...

She looks over to the barn. Hesitates, then begins walking
over to it.

INT. CONNELLY RANCH, BARN - NIGHT

Janna enters. The smells of animals, hay and barley brings
her a welcome-home smile.

She then sees her old family horse JACK(20) in a distant
stall. Janna approaches.

                         JANNA
                  Hey, Jackie... Remember me?

JACK, looking older than when Janna saw him last, none-the-
less, remembers her.

                         JANNA (CONT'D)
                  Yeah. You sure do, don't ya'. You
                  miss me?

Janna rubs his stiff and upright ears, gets the sleep out of
the old guy's eyes, rubs the top of his soft nose.

                         JANNA (CONT'D)
                  Yeah... Now you remember me don't
                  ya'" Don't ya'? Good boy, Jack.
                  Good boy.

She grabs a curry comb and starts brushing the horse.

                         BROCK (O.S.)
                  That's the wrong one.

Startled, Janna turns to see a handsome, looking BROCK
MCCARTY (30's) who appears from seemingly out of nowhere.

He's got drifter good-looks, and more than an air of gracious charm.

> BROCK (CONT'D)
> I'm sorry, ma'am. I didn't mean to
> startle you. I'm Dell's ranch hand,
> Brock. Brock McCarty.

> JANNA
> Oh. No, I, you just caught me off
> guard. I'm Dell's daughter, Janna
> Connelly.

Brock approaches.

> BROCK
> We've been expecting you at some
> point, just didn't know when.

> BROCK (CONT'D)
> That's a curry comb. Old Jack likes
> the body brush. The wood handle
> with the soft bristles.

Brock opens the pen gate and works the horse.

> JANNA
> Looks like he likes you.

> BROCK
> Well, he's a good old horse. He
> knows I mean him no harm. Feed him,
> wash him down. Been here about
> three months now. We're getting to
> know each other.

> JANNA
> He's looking at you all-right.

> BROCK
> Sometimes I think he's trying to
> talk to me.

> JANNA
> That's the beauty of horses. They
> don't even have to.

> BROCK
> If we had more of that these days,
> huh?

> JANNA
> Well, I should probably let my dad
> know I'm back.

INT. CONNELLY RANCH, FRONT ROOM - NIGHT

Dell lies prone in his old chair before the TV with a light knitted shawl covering his body.

Janna enters through the front door.

She moves quietly toward her father. An end table next to Dell reveals a whole host of awaiting medicines.

Janna places her travel pack on the nearby couch. Takes in the old house.

INT. CONNELLY RANCH, HOUSE - JANNA'S ROOM - NIGHT

She pushes through the door. For better or for worse, nothing changed - not an ounce of it.

Pictures of high school friends, bustling ranch and property photos, the same bedspread, left behind clothes in the closet - a photo of the three of them i.e., Dell, Janna and her beautiful mother - Adaline.

INT. CONNELLY RANCH HOUSE, FRONT ROOM - NIGHT

Janna moves close to Dell, takes a knee and reaches out for Dell's old, weathered hand. She feels it, it's familiarity.

Dell's eyes slowly open - his long-absent, daughter now before him.

                    DELL
               (fatigued)
          Hey, darlin'.

                    JANNA
          Hi, Dell.

                    DELL
          I thought it was today you'd be
          here. I tried to stay up. I guess
          it's been a while hasn't it?

                    JANNA
               (smiles)
          It has. Yeah.

                    DELL
          How long?

                    JANNA
          Seven-years.

                    DELL
          Long time.

                    JANNA
          Long time, Dell.

                    DELL
          You in the hot desert, and me out
          here in a frozen Dakota. Opposite
          ends, huh?

                    JANNA
               (smiles)
          We're here now.

INT. CONNELLY RANCH HOUSE, KITCHEN - LATER - NIGHT

Dell and Brock sit at the large, familiar kitchen table.

Janna jetties back and forth with a salad bowl, readies
coffee and another tin of her lasagna speciality.

                    JANNA
          Straight from the 41st Brigade
          Infantry, 201st division. My "Camp
          Black Horse" special. Lasagna, feta
          cheese, buttered french bread and a
          little caesar salad.

                    DELL
          Hey, this is something, Brock?
          Generally, we're left fighten' for
          the cheerios and the month-old milk
          to get 'em down.

                    JANNA
          Well, looks like you two've been
          living in this locker room long
          enough - now there's a new Sheriff
          in town. At least for a little
          while my family leave holds out.

                    BROCK
          With your dad's back, the bad
          winter...

                    JANNA
          So, the docs said "flutter"? Was it
          an atrial flutter? Those can be
          like an arrythmia if--

                    DELL (CON'T)
          It was nothing. Just a flutter. I
          was over doing it with Tom.
               (MORE)

                    DELL (CON'T) (CONT'D)
          Damn Old man Rafferty had enough of
          the winters. When the gun went off,
          it just caught me off-guard is all.
          (laughs) Hell, I thought that dun
          mare was going step on me and do me
          in.

                    JANNA
          Did he have any family left?

                    DELL
          I think he out-lived everybody
          around him. Big ranch. Alone.
          Barely even a mention of it in the
          paper. It's common. Isolation like
          that, old age, Dakota winters. Add
          all that up, a man can do some
          desperate things.

Brock grows uneasy - looks to change the subject.

                    BROCK
          So, if you don't mind me asking,
          how'd you find yourself patchin' up
          G.I.'s in a place like Afghanistan?

Dell and Janna - the $60,000 question.

                    JANNA
          (careful)
          Ah, well. At one point, we needed a
          little financial help around this
          place, during the summers through
          high school, I started to pick up
          part-time work in the local nursing
          facilities around Paxton. Once I
          graduated, well, for me, Paxton was
          a place to grow up...

                    DELL
          But not a place to stay.

A little tense. Some silence over a nice dinner. Brock breaks
the gulf between the two.

                    BROCK
          (broad charm)
          Well, you're back home now and
          we're all eating lasagna rather
          than cheerios and month-old milk.
          Coming from me, I'll take it.

We Hold:

INT. CONNELLY RANCH, HOUSE - JANNA'S ROOM - NIGHT

Janna enters and turns on a small lamp light. Her bedspread is covered with adolescent markings of horse figurines.

She pulls open the top of an old clothing drawer - she sees an old pair of her teenage pajamas.

                    JANNA
               (sighs)
          From America's battles.

She holds them against her waist.

EXT. CONNELLY RANCH, YARD - VARIOUS - NIGHT

The Connelly ranch house and barn is quiet. Dakota night sounds.

Janna's bedroom light gradually eases out.

                    JANNA (SIGHS)(V.O)
          To Spongebob Square-pants.

EXT. CONNELLY RANCH, ROAD - AFTERNOON - FOLLOWING - DAY

A Paxton County Sheriff's vehicle snakes its way up the long Connelly road.

INT. CONNELLY RANCH, KITCHEN - DAY

Late-afternoon, a very jet-lagged, Janna, finally up and awake, wattles in toward the coffee pot wearing her U.S. Military T-shirt on the top, and her teenage pajama bottoms below - 1/2 and 1/2.

She rumbles for the coffee grounds, pours water into the pot.

Dell and Brock's voices can be heard from outside the front porch.

                    DELL (O.S.)
          I want to try and get out there
          before it gets too late. Take a
          look at the herd.

                    BROCK (O.S.)
          That yearling with the group of
          fillies was only getting grass, but
          its weight doesn't look too bad.

EXT. CONNELLY HOUSE, FRONT PORCH - DAY

Janna steps out through the front door with coffee in hand - slow to wake.

                    JANNA
          Dell, you're not going to walk to
          the bathroom until we sit and go
          over your meds, check-out your BP.

                    BROCK
          Looks like the calvary has arrived.

                    JANNA
          Listen to Brock, Dell. Half-awake,
          but fully operational.

The tires of a Sheriff vehicle crackle over driveway rock approaching the Connelly home.

                    JANNA (CONT'D)
          Incoming.

                    DELL
          What's the Sheriff doing here?

Sherif Bostwickgets out of his vehicle along with Deputy Carl Haggen. Vehicle doors shut - both men approach the front porch.

                    SHERIFF BOSTWICK
          Morning, Dell

                    DELL
          Morning, Roger.

                    JANNA
          Deputy.

                    DEPUTY HAGGEN
          Miss Connelly.

                    SHERIFF BOSTWICK
             (to Janna)
          Don't think I've had the pleasure.

                    JANNA
          Janna Connelly. Just got in last
          night.

                    DELL
          Roger, Janna's an Air Force medic
          on leave to help me for a bit
          around the ranch.
                    (MORE)

                    DELL (CONT'D)
Don't let those pajama bottoms fool
you. And, this is my ranch hand,
Brock.

                    SHERIFF BOSTWICK
Well, thank you for your service,
ma'am.

                    DELL
What brings you out here, Roger?

                    SHERIFF BOSTWICK
Well, a couple of things. Wanted to
see how you were faring? Tom said
you almost got stepped on by that
horse out there when you collapsed.

                    DELL
I don't remember any of it. Was
sorry to hear about Hoag. Right in
front of you. Must have been tough.

                    SHERIFF BOSTWICK
Caught me by surprise, that's for
sure. Can you walk with me for a
minute?

                    DELL
Sure.

EXT. CONNELLY RANCH, CORRAL - DAY

Dell and the Sheriff walk at an easy pace.

                    SHERIFF BOSTWICK
Must be nice having your daughter
back for a bit?

                    DELL
It's been seven years since she's
left Paxton. She wasn't too keen on
staying. We've got some things to
work out, but I'm grateful.

The men stop, Dell leans on the corral.

                    DELL (CONT'D)
So, I'm sure you just didn't come
out to check on ole' Dell Connelly?

                    SHERIFF BOSTWICK
          I'm making the rounds letting the
          ranchers know there's some new
          guidelines that have come down the
          pike from the state legislature.

                    DELL
          Oh?

                    SHERIFF BOSTWICK
          The old man's suicide shook things
          up. His horses were in as bad as
          shape as he was. The UAPA got wind
          of it of course and ran with it.
          Farm Bureau is now on edge, it's
          all coming to a head where I'm
          going to find myself between the
          strong-arm animal lobbyists and the
          entire AG- community.

                    DELL
          What's all this mean to me?

                    SHERIFF BOSTWICK
          Been on the books for about a year
          now. Title 36. Rigorous spot
          inspections, felony enhancements
          for non-compliance, Vets now with
          enforcement power. Court can now
          act without informing owners, can
          rely simply on testimony, or an
          affidavit for seizure. Vets can
          destroy animals themselves if they
          see fit. Everything's upside down,
          Dell.

                    DELL
          I don't know one rancher, at least
          around here, who neglects or abuses
          his animals. (beat) Now, I see why
          you came out.

                    SHERIFF BOSTWICK
          Don't take it personal, Dell. I'm
          talking to all the ranchers.

                    DELL
          Thanks for taking the time, Roger.

EXT. CONNELLY RANCH, HOUSE - FRONT PORCH - DAY

Dell and the Sheriff approach as does Janna who now where's a
pair of jeans, Brock and Deputy Carl.

                         SHERIFF BOSTWICK
            So, by the mandate, we'll be out to
            all the ranches starting over the
            next few days with a local vet,
            checking on animals.

                         DELL
            I understand.

The Deputy hands a written-out, shortlist to Brock.

                         DEPUTY HAGGEN
            Some fencing, cracked tank heater,
            some mold in the barn stacks.

                         DELL
                 (beat)
            Looks like we got our marching
            orders.

INT. CONNELLY RANCH, KITCHEN - DUSK

Dell moves inside, cane clunking. Janna follows.

                         DELL
                 (agitated)
            I've known Roger for a long time.
            Something is now different bout
            him. He knows me better than that.
            If he thinks I'm the kind of man to
            hurt my horses he's lost his mind.

                         JANNA
            Brock told the Deputy the ranch is
            in good shape. Heard him myself.

                         DELL
            All of that should've been done
            already. I've had the same list for
            Brock the Deputy has for us - two
            months now. There's no excuses for
            that! I pay 'em well enough.

                         JANNA
            Dell, in all fairness Brock's been
            pullin' double-duty with you being
            laid-up.

                         DELL
            Then he should have been pullin'
            triple-duty! Our horses, cattle -
            you think things just wait for
            someone to get around to them?
                 (MORE)

                    DELL (CONT'D)
          The sale of our horses, yearlings,
          depends on our reputation. You lose
          that, we lose everything.

                    JANNA
          Calm down, Dell.

                    DELL
          Man walks up on another man's land -
          with accusations?

                    JANNA
          The Deputy said everyone was
          getting paid a visit.

Janna reaches for her backpack on the counter. She pulls out
her Blood Pressure (Sphygmomanometer).

                    DELL
          These ranchers out here are under
          enough pressure! Look at old man
          Rafferty! They came after him and
          he put himself down.

Janna approaches Dell while opening the BP arm-band.

                    JANNA
               (quietly)
          Dell, it's critical in recovery you
          try and keep yourself calm.

The ripping sound of the Velcro pulling apart triggers Dell's
a sharp.

                    DELL
          Stay away from me. I don't want my
          goddamn blood pressure to be taken!

Janna, shell-shocked, speechless. Back to square one - years
of pressure unlocked and fully on the table.

                    JANNA
               (composed)
          Okay.

She wraps up her blood pressure arm-strap - reaches for his
meds' on the kitchen counter.

                    JANNA (CONT'D)
          I didn't come all this way to be
          treated like I'm fourteen again,
          Dell.

Janna grabs her keys, phone and coat. She heads for the door.

                         JANNA (CONT'D)
                    (finally)
               Take two before you go to bed
               tonight.

EXT. CONNELLY RANCH, YARD - JANNA'S CAR - DUSK

Janna walks briskly with her phone in her hand. On the other
end - her good friend, Marla Orton.

                         JANNA (PHONE)
               Couple of drinks?

EXT. CONNELLY RANCH, BARN - DUSK

Brock, steps out from the barn and keeps his eye on Janna as
she tears down the Connelly road away from the main house.

He begins dialing on his flip phone.

INT. BULL-N-BREW SALOON - (LATER) - NIGHT

Atmosphere is light, locals scatter about - filled with ranch-
hands, cowboys and old-timers.

Janna, alone, waits on a bar stool for her friend. Bends the
BARTENDER (50'S) ear.

                         JANNA
                    (frustrated)
               A Captain in the U.S. Military,
               right? Doing my best to patch-up
               our G.I.'s on the front lines. And,
               when I get home for the first time
               in seven years, I'm reminded as
               quickly as I got there - nothing's
               changed! He turns me into that kid
               again who just wanted to get the
               hell off the farm.

Marla enters and sits.

                         JANNA (CONT'D)
               There you are.

                         MARLA
               Hiiiii...

                         JANNA
               Hiiiii...

They hug.

                    MARLA
          Sit.

They do.

                    MARLA (CONT'D)
          What happened out there? Dell go
          off the reservation?

                    JANNA
          Sheriff came out just to talk to -
          fencing issues, a few gaps near the
          road, field fixes. Normal post-
          Dakota-winter stuff.

                    MARLA
          Routine.

                    JANNA
          Right? But he got really upset
          about it. So, we walk back in the
          house. He starts in on the ranch-
          hand. "The guys not doing what he's
          suppose to be doing". And, by the
          way, the ranch-hand is hot. Another
          conversation, another time, but
          he's in my bunk house right now as
          we speak.

                    MARLA
          Dell.

                    JANNA
          Right, Dell. Okay, so he's going
          off on how the "Sheriff is
          targeting him" - he's "worried
          about the ranch's reputation". The
          selling of horses, bla, bla, bla. I
          thought his heart was going to blow
          again.

                    MARLA
          That doesn't sound like Dell at
          all. He knows the Sheriff.

                    JANNA
          I know. It's Hoag Rafferty. What
          happened to him - a little too
          close I think. Really spooked him.

Drinks arrive. Janna takes a good, deep sip.

                    MARLA
          Honey, Dell's scared right now.
          Animals are naturally thin from the
          winter. I see it everyday in my
          practice. He collapses in a field,
          gets a courtesy call from the law.
          Strength isn't what it was. It's
          all scary stuff.

                    JANNA
          It's just the way he looked at me.
          I saw that anger again.

                    MARLA
          Oh.

                    JANNA
          The stuff I thought I left forever.

                    MARLA
          From Kabul to Paxton County? Give
          yourself a little room, sweetie.
          You're decompressing, too.

                    JANNA
          When I got your call, I'd been on a
          full thirty-six hour shift. Was
          working on a young, cute, shot-up
          G.I. who was choking on a pool of
          his own blood. I didn't even reach
          for the paddles because I knew it
          wouldn't have mattered. He had a
          crush on me, too. Told me he had
          his eye on me for a while. I just
          held his hand along with his best
          friend and we whispered to each
          other about the date we were going
          to take someday. He just shut his
          eyes - died on the table. I
          couldn't save him. That's how I
          felt with Dell today - just, so far
          apart.

                    MARLA
          That's rough-stuff, honey.

                    JANNA
          I'm pretty tough that way, but
          seeing him so weak. I wasn't ready
          for that.

Marla's phone buzzes - the clinic.

                    JANNA (CONT'D)
          Take it, take it. I'll be alright.

                    MARLA (PHONE)
          Hello? (beat) Okay. I'll be right
          there.

                    JANNA
          You can't go?

                    MARLA
          I have to. Gelding got caught on a
          fence half way over it. Torn up,
          pretty good.

Marla gets up.

                    MARLA (CONT'D)
          Just breathe, breathe. You and Dell
          both are just working your own
          stubborn ways back home again.
          Coming in for that kind of
          approach, is always a little bumpy.

Marla exits.

Janna is stranded - checks her watch - no immediate interest
in going home right away.

She looks at a menu, then gets up and crosses the bar toward
an old jukebox.

She scrolls for something familiar.

She looks into the adjoining room to see Deputy Carl dressed
in civilian clothes playing pool with a friend.

MATT HUDSON (30's) handsome, with a cowboy charm, sits a few
chairs down from Janna away studying his phone.

Janna then sits at the end of the bar - music now fills the
Bull-in-Brew.

A fireball straight shot slides across the bar counter, slows
and lands right in front of Janna.

She looks to her left and sees a drunk looking man named
MASON (30'S) - the kind of guy who wildly over-estimates his
own physical persuasions.

Janna shoots back the drink with a flick of her forefinger.

                    JANNA
          Thanks, no.

Mason slides up anyway beside her with a stupid-looking look on his face - way too close for anybody's liking.

                    JANNA (CONT'D)
          I'm drinking alone tonight. Sorry.

                    MASON
               (stupid smiles)
          Didn't somebody write a song about
          that?

                    JANNA
          Yeah, I think they did. And, the
          second line is, and, "All by
          myself".

Mason leans closer - whiskey obnoxious.

                    MASON
          I like those songs you put on the
          jukebox. Dickie Peterson, The High-
          Lonesome.

                    JANNA
          What's your name?

                    MASON
          Mason. Mason Lang.

Mason works the hand down toward Janna's backside.

                    JANNA
          Well, Mason Lang, I kind of don't
          like you leaning on me, breathing
          on me for sure, and get your
          fucking hand away from my ass.
          Capeesh?

                    MASON
          Fiery! Why you gotta' be like that?

                    JANNA
          I know, I know. How dare I stand up
          for myself, God forbid. I'm such a
          bitch. I get it, I agree with you
          actually. Just go away. It's not
          just "no", it's "hell no". So bye
          now.

Deputy Carl approaches.

                    DEPUTY HAGGEN
          Mason. What the hell you doing?

                    MASON
          I got my quarters on the rail. Just
          waitin' for my name to be called -
          having a little fun, Carl.

                    DEPUTY HAGGEN
          Get up Mason. C'mon. Get up. I'm
          taking you home. Sorry, Janna.

Deputy Carl gets Mason to his feet and helps him along.

                    DEPUTY HAGGEN (CONT'D)
          Paxton still has 'em.

                    JANNA
          Thanks.

                    DEPUTY HAGGEN
          I'm sure I'll be seeing you.

                    MASON
               (last of the evening)
          I still like the songs you chose,
          little Janna.

                    JANNA
          Oh, Lord.

As Janna sits back down a new glass of whiskey slides over.

                    HUDSON
          A truly legendary flogging. My
          complements.

                    JANNA
          It's a gift. I happen to work with
          a lot of men. My father's one.

                    HUDSON
          Mind if I join you?

                    JANNA
          Yes.

                    HUDSON
          I won't breathe on you I promise.
          Unless you want me to of course,
          then, naturally I'm open for
          negotiations.

                    JANNA
          That's a novel opening line.

Janna lightens up - smiles.

                    HUDSON
          It's sad to drink alone.

                    JANNA
          I'm not sad.

                    HUDSON
               (winks)
          I was talking about me. Saddest
          cowboy in Paxton County. Can I tell
          you a joke?

                    JANNA
          Take a shot.

                    HUDSON
          Horse walks into a bar, seems kind
          of lonely, orders a few drinks,
          bartender says, "hey, why the long
          face?"

Janna's reluctantly charmed.

                    JANNA
          Yeah, okay. Ha.

Hudson sits on the chair next to her.

                    HUDSON
          I knew you'd like that one. Sure-
          fire crowd pleaser.

Hudson signals the Bartender to pour him one. Janna smiles
despite herself.

                    HUDSON (CONT'D)
          Name's Matt.

                    JANNA
          Janna.

                    HUDSON
          Pleasure.

                    JANNA
          Does this whole, easy-going
          southern cowboy-thing work for you?

                    HUDSON
               (killer smile)
          I have no idea what you're talking
          about but I like where it's going.

                         JANNA
              Fine, cowboy. Drinks. I can do
              drinks. But, look. I don't want you
              getting the wrong idea. Anything
              else, ain't happening.

                         HUDSON
                    (beat)
              Yes, ma'am.

INT. CONNELLY RANCH, BUNK HOUSE - NIGHT

Brock's belongings have been carefully packed and placed on a
small chair next to his bed.

He opens a drawer and pulls out the small UPS package sent to
him by **VETERINARIAN DR. VICTORIA MOREL**.

INT. HUDSON'S R & R MOTEL ROOM - NIGHT

A dim, small room.

Backing up toward the bed, Hudson and Janna passionately
kiss, deep into each other's arms, knocking sideways a small
motel table-lamp.

                         HUDSON
              You know, I don't usually... do
              this... on the first... date.

                         JANNA
                    (laughing)
              Shhhhhhhhh...

INT. CONNELLY RANCH, BUNK HOUSE - NIGHT

Brock carefully cuts open a small UPS package with the tip of
a very sharp knife.

He dumps out its contents onto his bedspread. We see a small
plastic bag of medical cue tips, along with a surgical facial
mask.

Brock lifts up a small vile which reads **PHF** - the infectious,
Potomac Horse Fever.

INT. HUDSON'S R & R MOTEL ROOM - NIGHT

Janna and Hudson pause for a momentary breath.

                         JANNA
              I don't either.

                    HUDSON
          Yes, ma'am.

She pushes him onto the bed and follows him down.

INT. CONNELLY RANCH, BARN - NIGHT

Brock carries a small bag of his personal things thrown over his shoulder. He's clearing out.

He stops at Jack's stall. The equine approaches Brock. Brock places the surgical mask over his face.

                    BROCK
          Hey, old boy. Looks like this is
          where I say my good-byes.

INT. HUDSON'S R & R MOTEL ROOM - NIGHT

Janna and Hudson, now on the bed, begin undressing the other, more kissing.

                    HUDSON
          I think old-Mason-boy dodged a
          bullet.

                    JANNA
          Why's that?

                    HUDSON
          He would've had his hands full with
          you.

INT. CONNELLY RANCH, BARN - NIGHT

Brock opens up the baggy of surgical cotton swabs.

He reaches into the **PHF** vile and then dips a Q-tip deep to the bottom of it - whirling it around.

                    BROCK
          Comes a time and age, best not to
          be a burden.

Brock navigates to the inside of Jack's nostrils.

                    BROCK (CONT'D)
              (beat)
          Every one and every thing becomes
          one, *eventually*.

EXT. HUDSON'S R & R MOTEL - FOLLOWING MORNING - DAY

Hudson's beaten-up blue Chevy flatbed is parked next Janna's rental.

INT. HUDSON'S R & R MOTEL - MORNING

Janna's eyes open - she's momentarily lost. She finds herself in an unfamiliar territory- laminate counters, a TV with a lock-wire on it.

                    JANNA
          What the hell?

Regretfully, it all floods back to her.

                    JANNA (CONT'D)
          Oh, no...

She turns back which only confirms her worst suspicions - Hudson lies half-naked and sleeping comfortably.

                    JANNA (CONT'D)
          Yep.

Janna reaches toward the side-table for her watch, squints at the early morning sun which cuts through the faded, pull-string curtains.

                    JANNA (CONT'D)
          Oh, my god.

She moves to get up but feels something like a "warm-leg" lying on top of hers'.

                    JANNA (CONT'D)
               (whispers)
          Shit.

She pulls back the bed sheet - looks down to see Hudson's leg draped over hers'.

                    JANNA (CONT'D)
          Shit. Shit. Shit.

EXT. CONNELLY RANCH, HOUSE - EARLY MORNING - DAY

Sheriff Bostwick's car and others are seen heading directly up the Connelly road.

INT. HUDSON'S R & R MOTEL - MORNING - DAY

Janna bends upright to reach for Hudson's ankle and foot - negotiating a noiseless escape.

42   42

Hudson, still in a deep sleep, grunts, makes a slow rolling turn with his body which pulls away all of the sheets covering Janna.

Exposed from the waist up, she crosses her arms to cover herself.

                    JANNA
               (whisper)
          Hey?!

EXT. CONNELLY RANCH, HOUSE - MORNING

Sheriff Bostwick and Deputy Carl stand near veterinarian, DR. VIRGINIA MOREL (40s-50s).

She orders around two of her VET TECHS.

Dell, wearing his robe, alone, stands in the middle of the activity - disoriented, confused.

                    DELL
          Brock? BROCK?

INT. HUDSON'S R & R MOTEL - MORNING

Janna moves to the side of the bed - slips on her shirt over her head, pulls on her boots.

She looks over to Hudson - deep sleep. Slips into her boots - slowly, one at a time. Janna steps for the door.

                    HUDSON (O.S.)
               (beat)
          Feel like little breakfast? I make
          a mean bacon and egg scramble.

Janna turns.

                    JANNA
          Morning Matt.

Hudson gets up onto his shoulder - relaxed, broad smile.

                    HUDSON
          Morning, Miss Kabul. Now, you
          weren't just going to run out now
          were you?

EXT. CONNELLY RANCH, FIELD - DAY

Dr. Morel takes photos of animals, water troughs, down fencing. Assistant Technicians spot the field behind her.

A VET TECH approaches Dr. Morel.

> VET TECH
> We got something in the barn you're
> going to want to see.

EXT. PAXTON COUNTY ROAD - MORNING - DAY

Janna drives. Now a bit more relaxed. Turns on the radio -
local news - Janna, alert, awake, interested.

Phone on speaker phone. (Friend Marla's outgoing message -
Beep)

> JANNA
> Hi... It's me... You are so in
> trouble for leaving me alone last
> night. Call me.

INT. CONNELLY RANCH, BARN - MORNING - DAY

The Vet Tech leads Dr. Morel and Sheriff Bostwick toward the
back stall.

> VICTORIA MOREL
> What is it?

> VET TECH
> Back stall. Old draft horse to the
> left.

They arrive at Jack's stall. Jack looks uneasy, frothing at
the mouth and nose.

> VET TECH (CONT'D)
> Look. Ears hanging down, we checked
> his nose and nasal passages.

> VICTORIA MOREL
> Creamy discharge. Elevated
> respiratory.

Dr. Morel places her stethoscope against Jack's chest.

> VICTORIA MOREL (CONT'D)
> A lot of pinging.

> SHERIFF BOSTWICK
> What's that mean?

> VICTORIA MOREL
> Possible Herpesvirus, or Potomac
> Horse Fever. What other horses have
> been in this stall?

INT. CONNELLY RANCH, KITCHEN - DAY

Dell, motionless. Sherif Bostwicksits soberly across from
him. The news has been had.

                    SHERIFF BOSTWICK
               (long beat)
          I don't know what to say, Dell. The
          foal has to be quarantined as well.
          Vet said some sort of virus. I know
          what this does to a man, to
          anybody.

                    DELL
          That horse has been part of this
          ranch and family even before the
          accident. That was Adaline's horse,
          Roger. She had him as a foal.

                    SHERIFF BOSTWICK
          Yeah. Doing the right thing is
          rarely doing the easy thing.
          Looking out for the rest of your
          herd, that's the right thing.

                    DELL
          I know it is.

                    SHERIFF BOSTWICK
          Listen, I know it's impossible. I'm
          your friend. I wouldn't ask you to
          do it unless I'd do it myself for
          ya'.

                    DELL
          No. Even if it is just a horse, I
          want him to be looking at a
          familiar face before he goes. He
          deserves at least that.

The Sheriff reaches for his Beretta 92 Series and places it
on the table.

                    SHERIFF BOSTWICK
          The safety is beneath the trigger
          on the grip. I'll wait here for
          you.

EXT. CONNELLY RANCH, YARD - DAY

Dell walks across the yard toward the barn with the Sheriff's
gun in his hand - whiskered, tired, broken, the longest walk
of his life.

Deputy Carl, empathetic, watches all of it as Dell crosses the yard for the grisly chore.

INT. CONNELLY RANCH, BARN - DAY

Barn door opens. Dell in his robe slowly walks down to the last stall.

The horse listlessly approaches the gate and rubs his long snout up against Dell's chest.

                    DELL
               (near whispers)
          Come here, old boy. How'd you get
          so sick, huh?

Dell just spend some time rubbing Jack's face and ears.

                    DELL (CONT'D)
          If I had to write down all the
          things you've been to me, and
          Adaline, Janna... I'd be forced to
          write a whole book on you, Jack.

Dell rubs the horse under his neck and ears with his left hand, gun held out of view with his right.

                    DELL (CONT'D)
          Vanities and dust, I guess.

Dell moves closer to Jack's limping ear.

                    DELL (CONT'D)
               (whispers)
          I'm gonna' put ya', on the back
          quarter, near that great-oak-shade
          you liked so much when the summers
          came. And, whenever I visit you out
          there, I'll always think about what
          you've meant to us. I'll have it
          written out, and it'll read; "Here
          lies the one who loved us all, and
          in return, the one who was loved as
          much. And, no matter how deep your
          sleep, I will always hear you, old
          friend - and not even death will
          keep your spirit from running
          freely in my fields".

INT. CONNELLY RANCH, KITCHEN - DAY

Sherif Bostwickjust sits, spins his spoon in a cup of coffee. Then, the sound of one muffle gun-shot.

Moments later, Dell comes back in, sits and places the
Sheriff's weapon on the table.

                    SHERIFF BOSTWICK
          By the rest of your herd, you did
          the right thing, Dell.

EXT. CONNELLY RANCH, FRONT PORCH - LATER - DAY

The ranch is quiet. Dell is alone still wearing his robe from
the morning sitting in his chair - expressionless.

EXT. CONNELLY RANCH, YARD - DAY

Janna's car comes back up the road. She pulls in, turns off
the motor, and opens her door.

From the yard, she sees Dell sitting alone staring off in
space. She walks over to him.

                    JANNA
          Dell?

EXT. CONNELLY RANCH, HOUSE - FRONT PORCH - DAY

Janna approaches, Dell doesn't move - catatonic, merely,
stares out before him.

                    JANNA
          What happened out here?

Dell doesn't answer. Janna looks around - eerily quiet.

                    JANNA (CONT'D)
          Where's Brock?

Sensing the worst,

                    JANNA (CONT'D)
          No.

Janna bolts to the farmhouse.

INT. CONNELLY RANCH, BUNK HOUSE - DAY

Janna enters. He's cleared out. Empty. Not even a trace. She
turns and flies out of the room.

EXT. CONNELLY RANCH, YARD - DAY

Janna sprints to the barn.

INT. CONNELLY RANCH, BARN - DAY

Janna opens the barn door fearing the worst. She cautiously walks to the last stall.

                    JANNA
          No... No... please, no...

She approaches the stall. Janna clutches the stall gate board. The worst imagine - all too real.

                    JANNA (CONT'D)
          Oh, god... Oh, god...

EXT. CONNELLY RANCH, YARD - DAY

Moments later, Janna emerges.

Ravaged by the loss, Janna makes her way over to her father, who continues to sit and stare.

EXT. CONNELLY RANCH, HOUSE - FRONT PORCH - DAY

Janna kneels and places her head on Dell's lap. Tears come - slow to build, forever to flow.

Dell reaches out and places his comforting hand over her head and shoulders for as long as it's going to take.

                    JANNA
          I'm sorry, Dell. I'm sorry I wasn't
          here.

INT. CONNELLY RANCH, KITCHEN - FOLLOWING MORNING - DAY

Janna, focused, sits fully dressed at the kitchen table. She combs through the list left behind by the Sheriff.

Dell enters the kitchen. Pours a coffee.

                    DELL
          Morning.

                    JANNA
          Morning.

                    JANNA (CONT'D)
          See, they took Roan too?

                    DELL
          Yeah.

                    JANNA
          Do we even know where?

                    DELL
          I think Roger said they'd let us
          know.

                    JANNA
          Boy, they just come in and leave a
          wake of abuse don't they?

                    DELL
          Yeah.

                    JANNA
               (reads)
          Reading their notices. Lack of care
          for livestock, pasture too short,
          feed purchase records, inaccessible
          roads.

Dell sits.

                    JANNA (CONT'D)
          You take your meds'?

                    DELL
          In the bathroom.

                    JANNA
          How're you feeling?

                    DELL
          Tired. Grumpy. Pissed-off. You?

                    JANNA
          Tired, grumpy and even more pissed-
          off. Going over their notices,
          they're making us sound like
          accused criminals. I've been cross-
          referencing your ranch records with
          the complaints. None of this adds
          up.

                    DELL
          What do you see?

                    JANNA
          Lack of care for livestock but they
          don't cite any. Incomplete feed
          records, but I'm looking at them
          right here. We're still two months
          out from even getting close to low.
          Roads out because they're still
          frozen. I mean, really?

                    DELL
          I've been a bit slow since the
          hospital but none of that sounds
          right.

                    JANNA
          Tell me more about Hoag Rafferty.
          What happened to him?

Dell sits.

                    DELL
          Hard winter of course. 80 plus
          years-old. He had a ranch-hand who
          left sometime in January. Really
          hurt him.

                    JANNA
          Ranch hand left, huh?

                    DELL
          Tom and I went out that morning to
          help him get some animals fed.
          Roger was out there talking to him.
          They went out to the barn. I guess
          he was going to put down a horse,
          but turned the gun on himself.
          That's when I went down - about
          all I remember.

Janna reaches for her Blood Pressure wrap. Dell, willingly
extends his arm. Janna wraps it and pumps it up.

                    DELL (CONT'D)
          I'm sorry about yesterday. I guess
          it's all gotten to me.

                    JANNA
          Me, too. It's gotten to me as well.

She unwraps the arm wrap.

                    JANNA (CONT'D)
          Little high but you're okay. I'm
          going to go out the barn, get
          tissue sample from Jack, then, get
          out there to Marla's clinic.

                    DELL
          Why?

                    JANNA
              (beat)
          I want to check something out.

INT. MARLA'S CLINIC - DAY

Marla inspects Jack's skin specimen - carefully sealing it.

                    MARLA
          I'll send this out and have it back
          in a few days. When I get it, I'll
          come out and check on some of the
          animals.

                    JANNA
          I just don't get it.

Janna leans against an exam table in the background.

                    MARLA
          Title 36 is making it hard on
          everybody.

                    JANNA
          What's that?

                    MARLA
          State laws they put in about a year
          ago. More rigourous.

                    JANNA
          Like what?

                    MARLA
          They've made it, where there's no
          liability of the accuser?

                    JANNA
          Huh?

                    MARLA
          Piss off the wrong neighbor, that
          can cause you a lot of trouble. A
          person can falsely accuse someone
          of neglect, causing them financial
          hardships in order to prove their
          innocence. Cost them nothing. Costs
          you to defend yourself everything.
          I hear about all of it in here.
          Welcome back to the Badlands of
          Nor' Dakoda.

                    JANNA
          Go away for a little while and
          everything gets turned up down. No
          wonder Dell is stressed.

>   MARLA
>   How's Mr. Beautiful man in the bunk
>   house? How's he taking it?

>   JANNA
>   Mr. Beautiful bunk house man - he
>   be' gone, too! Not a trace. Just up
>   and left. I need someone out there
>   Dell can count on. I don't know how
>   long the Air Force is going to let
>   me slide.

>   MARLA
>   I gotta' guy. He was just in here
>   for a client. Looking for a place
>   to work and sleep.

>   JANNA
>   Really?

>   MARLA
>   Go to the Krol's Diner. His name is
>   Hudson. I'll call him, will explain
>   everything so he knows.

EXT. CONNELLY RANCH, HILLSIDE OAK - DAY

Below a large oak, Dell stares out across the valley below -
points to some LOCAL HELPERS to begin digging.

>   DELL
>   Pointing this way. Under the shade.
>   Right here will be fine.

EXT. KROL'S DINER - DAY

Empty restaurant.

Janna sits at a cushioned booth facing the door. She's been
waiting a while now - looks at her watch.

Waitress comes by and fills her coffee cup.

>   JANNA
>   Thanks. I'll take the check, too.
>   He's not showing up.

But someone does show-up - in through the glass doors, comes
walking in her R & R motel cowboy-lover, Hudson.

Janna's jaw drops. He sees her - caught cold - holds a minute
- doesn't bat an eye - turns to the counter and sits.

                         JANNA (CONT'D)
          Shit.

Janna gets up and crosses over - the long perp walk.

MORE - THE COUNTER

Hudson just acts like she doesn't exist. She approaches and
Hudson keeps his eyes fixed straight ahead.

                         JANNA (CONT'D)
          I'm sorry, Matt. I didn't mean to
          run out on you yesterday morning.
          I guess this town is smaller that I
          than I remembered. I'm really
          sorry.

                         HUDSON
          No problem. I generally don't do
          that to people, but, all good.

          I have an interview, so if you
          don't mind?

                         JANNA
          Oh, sure. Okay, yeah, okay.

Janna turns and makes her way back to her booth. Her phone
rings - it's Marla.

                         MARLA (PHONE V.O.)
          He show up, yet?

                         JANNA
          No... But I did run into the guy
          who took me to the Ritz R & R.

                         MARLA (PHONE V.O.)
          Nooooo...

                         JANNA
          He's sitting at the counter. This
          is embarrassing. He's not happy.

                         MARLA (PHONE V.O.)
          The only thing worse than waking up
          the first day is seeing him on the
          second.

                         JANNA
          I've been waiting. What's this guy
          look like again?

Janna looks over to Hudson who keeps to himself, reading a menu.

> MARLA (PHONE V.O.)
> Hudson. Lanky guy, short hair, blue
> eyes, angular face kind of - about
> 6-1, 6-2.

> JANNA
>   (beat)
> I gotta' go.

Janna gets up from her booth and approaches Hudson. With the phone in his ear, he turns to see Janna turning off her own phone.

> JANNA (CONT'D)
> Matt.

> HUDSON
> Yeah?

> JANNA
> You're last name wouldn't be
> "Hudson" by any chance would it?

EXT. CONNELLY RANCH, FENCES / MUD FIELD - DAY

Janna and Hudson walk up a small knoll which overlooks all of the Connelly property.

> HUDSON
> Wow... All this yours'?

> JANNA
> My family's, my fathers'.

> HUDSON
> Beautiful.

> JANNA
> Had over fifty horses at one point
> when I was a kid. I didn't see
> myself doing it my whole life like
> he does. My mom passed in a drunk
> driver's accident when I was
> fourteen. I had to go to work, find
> a way to bring in some money. I
> didn't see any way out really so I
> joined up, using my nursing
> credential I got here. That was a
> big problem for Dell.
>   (MORE)

                    JANNA (CONT'D)
He had a heart attack a few weeks
back so I took emergency family
leave to come back here - help out,
make sure he was okay.

                    HUDSON
Is he?

                    JANNA
I don't know. He hired some guy -
he just took off. Too much for him,
who knows?

                    HUDSON
I hear a lot of that.

Hudson walks over to some fencing. Inspects it.

                    HUDSON (CONT'D)
This is a patch job. Your guy--

                    JANNA
Brock.

                    HUDSON
Right. He just twisted some wire to
hold the paddock rather than
replace the length. Sloppy.

                    JANNA
So it was deliberate?

                    HUDSON
Maybe some of it. Or he's just a
lazy. When a job is too big, I've
seen some fellows just shirk off
everything.

                    JANNA
Marla is coming over with Jack's
test results, and I want to
introduce you to Dell. So, we're in
agreement? Right?

                    HUDSON
I think so. The money's fine, the
bunk house is fine. I do have just
one request.

                    JANNA
What's that?

                    HUDSON
          If you have an itch, and you need
          some scratchin', and you come-a-
          knockin', I'm gonna' ask that you
          at least know my whole name before
          we begin commencing. I'm a cowboy
          with principles.

                    JANNA
          You're going to make me pay aren't
          you?

                    HUDSON
               (smiles)
          Just a little bit.

EXT. CONNELLY RANCH, CORRAL - DAY

Marla leads Janna, Dell, and Hudson to the gate of the
corral.

                    MARLA
          It came back. He was sick.

                    JANNA
          What was it?

                    MARLA
          Potentially-fatal febrile illness
          affecting horses caused by the
          intracellular bacterium - big word -
          Neorickettsia risticii. Potomac
          Fever, or, better known as, Shasta
          River Crud.

                    DELL
          We've never had that before.

                    MARLA
          It happens. Accidental ingestion of
          infected adult insects, who fly
          into barns and die in stalls,.
          Get's eaten up in the hay. I feel
          bad for the horse, but he may have
          died anyway. You did the right
          thing, Dell.

Marla expertly runs her hand down the leg of a horse while
Hudson, Dell and Janna looks on.

                    MARLA (CONT'D)
          He's a bit thin, but so are most of
          the horses across Paxton.
               (MORE)

                    MARLA (CONT'D)
There's nothing here that screams
abuse or neglect to me.

                    HUDSON
     (to Janna)
There you go.

                    JANNA
Were you the one that inspected
Hoag Rafferty's horses?

                    MARLA
No. That was Victoria Morel. They
called her to look at Hoag's
animals.

Marla looks from Hudson to Janna.

                    DELL
What happens next?

                    MARLA
Let's make it official. I'll assess
the entire herd. I can set up a
feeding and exercise plan to bring
these animals back into shape.

                    DELL
Hudson, looks like your timing is
spot on.

EXT. SHOPPING CENTER - DAY

Janna and Hudson load up feed supplies in the back of
Hudson's truck.

Parked an aisles over and out of view, is Sheriff Bostwick.
Deputy Carl Haggen returns to the patrol vehicle with two
coffees.

                  DEPUTY HAGGEN
Here you go, Sheriff.

Steiner takes his coffee.

                  SHERIFF BOSTWICK
Carl, why don't you go over there
and casually see what you can find
out.

Carl looks up and sees Janna and apparently the new man.

                  DEPUTY HAGGEN
Yeah, who is that?

Carl keeps his coffee and continues walking over the Hudson's flatbed.

EXT. PARKING LOT - DAY

Carl approaches. He eyeballs Hudson. Janna looks up to see the familiar deputy.

                    JANNA
          Oh, hi, Carl.

                    DEPUTY HAGGEN
          Getting some feed, huh?

                    JANNA
          Yep. Knocking down that list you
          gave us. Want to be compliant.
          Don't want to be caught short next
          time you come out.

                    DEPUTY HAGGEN
          Good deal.

                    HUDSON
          I'm Matt Hudson. Nice meeting you.

Hudson extends an open hand. Carl is slow to reach for it - fumbling with the coffee.

                    DEPUTY HAGGEN
          Yeah. Of course.

                    JANNA
          Matt's the new hand we hired since
          Brock left. He'll be picking up
          where Brock left off.

                    DEPUTY HAGGEN
          What happened to him?

                    JANNA
          Nobody knows.

                    DEPUTY HAGGEN
          I hear that a lot.

                    JANNA
          Well, good seeing Carl. I'm sure
          we'll see you out there!

Hudson and Janna get into Hudson's truck, back up and pull out. Janna waves as Carl simply stands there.

He turns and makes his way back to the patrol vehicle.

INT. SHERIFF PATROL CAR - DAY

Carl opens the door and slides in the passenger seat - the Sheriff waits to hear.

                    SHERIFF BOSTWICK
          What'd you find out?

                    DEPUTY HAGGEN
          Looks like Miss Connelly hired a
          new ranch hand, a Matt Hudson.

                    SHERIFF BOSTWICK
          New ranch hand, huh?

                    DEPUTY HAGGEN
          Yeah. I used to know from her high
          school. Didn't pay much attention
          to her back then.

                    SHERIFF BOSTWICK
          I liked the way you handled that,
          Carl. You're learning.

EXT. CONNELLY RANCH, BARN - DAY

Janna and Hudson unload the supplies. Dell walks up to a nearby fence and hooks his cane over the railing.

                    DELL
          We got the list of conditions from
          the State Attorney.

Janna and Hudson join Dell at the fence as he pulls out an official looking LIST. They look it over.

                    JANNA
          Underweight horses, well that's
          debatable.

                    HUDSON
          Fence repair, brush clearing,
          standing water, yeah we saw that
          already.

                    JANNA
             (reading)
          Wait. Replace bad wiring in the de-
          icing element in the water troughs?
          Where are those?

                    DELL
                (points)
        That one is way out in the north
        field.

EXT. CONNELLY RANCH, FIELD - DAY

Janna, Dell and Hudson approach a water trough along the
fence line.

Hudson bends over.

                    HUDSON
        Look at this. Exposed electrical
        wiring. I've seen animals get
        electrocuted by this.

Hudson opens a panel at the side of the trough revealing some
corroded, exposed wires.

                    HUDSON (CONT'D)
        Looks like the ice got in here and
        corroded the connections. I mean
        that happens all the time.

                    JANNA
        How did they know?

                    DELL
        Everybody has de-icers. If you
        don't put a heater in there, the
        water troughs freeze up in the
        winter. Horses get no water.

                    JANNA
        No, I mean. Did you see Morel or
        her people go out this way? Or the
        Sheriff?

                    HUDSON
        The panel was rusted shut. Nobody's
        been here.

                    JANNA
        There's no tire marks, or shoe
        prints in the mud.

                    DELL
        I didn't see 'em go this far.

INT. CONNELLY RANCH, HOUSE - DAY

Dell sits in his chair. Hudson leans against the wall nearby.
Janna paces from left to right.

                    JANNA
          Don't you see? It was Brock. The
          inspectors didn't go out to the
          north field but they included it in
          their report and it reads here on
          the State's Attorney's own
          stationary.

                    HUDSON
          So, how is this Brock-guy, tied all
          the way up to the State's
          Attorney's office?

                    DELL
          No way of proving that.

                    JANNA
          I think we might need some help.
          Legal help.

                    HUDSON
              (clears his throat)
          I may know a guy.

INT. PHARMACY - DAY

Janna steps up to the counter. PHARMACIST (60's) approaches.

                    JANNA
          Dell Connelly. I'm his daughter,
          Janna. Picking up from Dr. Kruger.

Janna looks down to a nearby newspaper rack. The Paxton
Gazette - Headline reads; **RANCHER'S CRUELTY.**

Janna picks it up and begins reading.

65   *"Connelly Family Ranch were given official notice from the* 65
      North Dakota State Attorneys General's Office..."

INT. HUDSON'S TRUCK - DAY

Janna opens Hudson's door clutching Dell's meds and newspaper-
jumps inside the truck.

                    JANNA
              Let's go. Go!

INT. VIN'S OFFICE - DAY

ATTORNEY VIN SCURLOCK (30's) sits behind his yard-sale oak
desk facing Hudson and Janna.

He finishes the article from the Paxton Gazette.

                    VIN
Doesn't take a genius to see what's
happening here. It's this new law -
Statute 45-15. They couldn't get it
through the voters, so they did an
end-run and shoved right through
the legislature.

                    JANNA
But why?

                    VIN
Question of the day, isn't it? It's
the animal rights groups with their
lobbying power. Listen, don't
repeat this, but do you know how
much money is donated to those
folks when they show a commercial,
or run an ad-buy with a lonely dog
coopt up in a dog pen? It's
horrifying, I get it. But do know
what's even more horrifying?

                    JANNA
What's that?

                    VIN
The salaries that are paid by a
those "NON-PROFITS" to there senior
executives. Six figures and more.
That's right, Mattie. And, now they
have a lock on the states and how
laws are being implemented. Don't
kid yourself! The problem is, many
animal rights groups are wolves in
sheep clothing, pretending to be
animal welfare. They don't care
anything for the animals, most
money is spent in high salaries,
fancy offices and lobbying. That's
the God's honest truth.

                    JANNA
I'm getting it now.

                    VIN
"The economy is bad and more houses
are in foreclosure? Well, let's
create a fund for pets affected
by foreclosure!"

                    JANNA
Why would they want to take
rancher's horses?

                    VIN
         Lot's of reasons. Reasons that
         aren't so nice.

                    HUDSON
         So, what does she do?

                    VIN
         You're headed in the right
         direction so far. You need to show
         'em we're complying. So I'll get
         the vet assessment from your pal
         Dr. Marla, the care plan for the
         horses and various other papers
         together and get them ready. Once
         its done, you and I can hand-walk
         it over to the State Attorney.
         It'll buy you some time and free
         ya'll up to get that ranch in
         order.

                    JANNA
              (beat)
         What's it going to cost me?

INT. CONNELLY RANCH, HOUSE - DAY

Dell on the phone. Dell and Hudson walk in the ranch house.

                    DELL (PHONE)
         But its hay from my land and we had
         an agreement. Tom? Tom! Tom Gardner
         just hung up on me.

Dell puts down the phone.

                    JANNA
         What is it?

                    DELL
         He's saying he doesn't have any hay
         for me this year.

EXT. TOM GARDNER'S FRONT PORCH - DAY

Dell and Janna approach Tom Gardner's front door. Dell knocks
- Tom answers.

                    TOM
         Now listen, Dell, we've known each
         other for a long time.

                    DELL
         Thirty-five years.

                    TOM
          Hello, Janna.

                    JANNA
          Mr. Gardner.

                    TOM
          Janna, like I told your pa, I'm
          afraid I just don't have any to
          sell.

                    DELL
          Well, Tom, we pulled hay from your
          barn for Hoag, a few weeks ago. You
          and I we're shoveling out as much
          as he needed.

                    TOM
          The extra hay I did have, been sold
          since then. New farmer over in
          Fargo took all I had, paid top-
          dollar.

                    DELL
               (quietly)
          I've been buying hay from you, this
          time of year, every year now for
          the last 20 since you first bought
          your ranch.

                    TOM
          That's about right.

                    JANNA
               (beat)
          What's the change, Mr. Gardner? You
          knew Dell would be calling you?

Tom's got nothin'. Janna reaches for the Gazette article from
her back pocket.

                    JANNA (CONT'D)
          Is this actually the truth of it,
          sir? Is this why you won't sell
          your hay to us? People will think
          its your hay that contaminated the
          Connelly Ranch? Jack was put down
          for Potomac Fever. I'm guessing it
          was just a mosquito that dropped a
          larva into the stall. He ate it up,
          got sick. Had nothing to do with
          the quality of your product coming
          from the Gardner Farm.

RUTH GARDNER (60'S) steps out of the house - a bit disgusted from what she's hearing.

                    TOM
          Go back inside, Ruth.

                    RUTH
          I'm not going inside, Tom. These
          people, your friends, deserve the
          truth. You owe 'em, that.

Quiet on the porch between the men

                    RUTH (CONT'D)
          Look Dell in the eye, and tell him.

                    TOM
          Title 38 has us all spooked. Every
          rancher out here is hiding from the
          Sheriff and his posse.

                    RUTH
          Tom's afraid that what happened to
          you could happen to us, too.
          Sheriff visits, articles.

                    TOM
          I'm going to have to put some
          distance between us to protect the
          ranch, Dell.

                    DELL
          I see.

                    TOM
               (beat)
          Reputation is everything. You know
          that. Any whiff of fever, or grass
          sickness coming off my hay, I'd be
          finished. I'm sorry, Dell.

EXT. CONNELLY RANCH, CORRAL - LATER - DAY

Two horses stand in the corral. Hudson offers Janna the lead rope.

                    HUDSON
          I got some calls out on those
          yearlings. See if we can get some
          buyers lined up.

She takes it. Hudson steps to the other horse to attach the other lead.

                        JANNA
        Okay.

Both stand back to back and slowly circle, urging the horses
to trot around them - circles and endless circles - thinking,
figuring - assessing.

MONTAGE - MORE - VARIOUS:

EXT. CONNELLY RANCH, FIELDS / CORRAL - HOUSE - DAY

Days, nights, other days...

Breakfasts, Dinners, Lunches... All on the move to pick up
the pace around the ranch.

Janna brushes, feeds and works the horses like she used to.

Hudson works to lift and clean out a water trough - water
pours out - he checks the wiring, the de-icer - scrubbing the
trough.

Bags of feed thrown into the back of his flatbed. He carries
bags of feed and grain - gets the animals ready for feeding.

Janna once-more, sits Dell down at the table and monitors
Dell's blood pressure.

Hudson lasso's field posts, feed cans, sitting saddles.

Hudson, pulls down old siding, reconstitutes the new. He
enters the corral - takes a lunge rope, leads a horse around
the corral - Janna rubs down the tendons of another.

More...

INT. PAXTON COUTHOUSE - DAY

Janna and Vin turn over Marla's animal physical assessment.

INT. CONNELLY RANCH, BARN - AFTERNOON - DAY

Janna shovels a stall, looks up to see Dell carrying a basket
of BLACK-EYED-SUSANS ready for planting.

                        DELL
        I thought we'd get some color back
        around here.

                        JANNA
        Mom's favorites.

                    DELL
          (smiles)
     Beautiful, aren't they? Bout time
     we have something of her around
     here again.

INT. VIN'S OFFICE - DAY

Janna and Hudson sit before Vin.

                    JANNA
     The court can act without notice?

                    VIN
     It goes back to the existing law
     again, I'm afraid. I'm going to
     prepare an injunction in case they
     do move on the ranch. If they do
     come, that's all we have.

INT. DINER - DAY

Janna and Hudson sit. Janna goes through her checkbook.

                    JANNA
     Well, this is pitiful. Looks like
     I'll be tappin' out my credit
     union. So much for buying a place
     of my own.

                    HUDSON
          (smiles)
     I'll get the tip.

EXT. CONNELLY RANCH, FIELD - NIGHT

Under the dark starlit sky, Janna sits alongside Hudson on a
rolling knoll which overlooks the Connelly property.

                    JANNA
          (beat)
     Sometimes, I'd find a place,
     between shifts, and I'd sit out
     there, just by myself, when all the
     work was done. I'd just look up and
     think of this place where we're
     sitting now. Nobody really thinks
     about, but the stars there are the
     same ones here. I'd hold my hands
     over the sides of my face, like
     this, and just stare straight up.
     Made me feel like I was right here.
          (MORE)

                         JANNA (CONT'D)
          One-time, there was a young girl,
          inside the camp, younger than me,
          crying, all alone. Her mother had
          been hit, either by us, or them but
          we took her in. The young Afghan
          girl was looking up, just like I
          was. And, then she looked to me
          after all that time. Didn't say a
          word. She was just thinking about
          her mother. She turned back up, and
          started staring back up at the
          stars again, tears streaming down
          her face, scared, just staring like
          we're doing now. I saw she was as
          tied to her home, as much as I was
          tied to mine. And, even though I
          ran from this place with everything
          I had, I find myself running back
          to it with everything I have left.
          Just like that young girl who was
          worried about her mother, I'd think
          of Dell. The place I hated, is now
          the place that's saving me. Funny
          isn't it?

Hudson adjusts the blanket over shoulders.

EXT. INTERSTATE DINER - FOLLOWING DAY - 6 AM - DAY

Rural County North Dakota.

Isolated roadside diner - the kind of place you go out of
your way to have a private conversation.

A single car roars by

INT. INTERSTATE DINER - DAY

Tight on two men. Sheriff Bostwick, out of uniform, sits
opposite of RUSSEL ASHTON (50'S), UAPA animal rights
lobbyist.

The Sheriff turns his spoon round and round in his cup of
coffee.

                         SHERIFF BOSTWICK
                    (measured)
          You know it's actually the sugar
          that raises one's cholesterol that
          gives people heart disease?

Russel thumbs through a folder of dozens of photos of
ranches, horse herds, transport trailers, ranch owners.

                    RUSSEL ASHTON
               (all files)
          Hm, hmm. You know all these
          ranchers in these parts personally?

                    SHERIFF BOSTWICK
          Most of 'em. If I don't, I'm happy
          to introduce myself.

                    RUSSEL ASHTON
          How many head?

                    SHERIFF BOSTWICK
          Couple thousand.

                    RUSSEL ASHTON
          That's a lot of dog food.

                    SHERIFF BOSTWICK
          I'll need the political cover -
          have to get firm with a few in my
          own way.

                    RUSSEL ASHTON
               (agreeing)
          I have no idea what you're
          referring to, Sheriff.

The WAITRESS approaches.

                    WAITRESS
          Sorry to have kept you waiting.
          Have you decided?

We pull back to reveal Dr. Victoria Morel and her strong-arm
man, Brock. Russel looks to the group.

                    RUSSEL ASHTON
          I think we have.

INT. CONNELLY RANCH, JANNA'S ROOM - EARLY MORNING - DAY

Janna's CELL PHONE rings. She fumbles bringing it to her ear.

                    JANNA
               (grumbling)
          You always call so early.

                    MARLA (PHONE V.O.)
          It's happening, Janna! They're on
          the move to your ranch. I'm on my
          way!

EXT. RURAL ROAD - DAY

Transport trucks make their way to the Connelly Ranch.

INT. CONNELLY RANCH, JANNA'S ROOM - EARLY MORNING - DAY

Janna quickly gets dressed.

> JANNA
> Dell! DELL! WAKE UP!

Janna calls Vin. He picks up.

> VIN (V.O.)
> Hello?

> JANNA
> They're on they're way. Get going!

> VIN (V.O.)
> When you get the seizure order,
> send me a picture from your phone.
> I'll try and buy some time.

EXT. PAXTON, COURTHOUSE - MORNING - DAY

Putting on his BOLO TIE, tucking in his shirt, Vin makes his
way into the court house building.

INT. CONNELLY RANCH, HOUSE - MORNING - DAY

Janna hurries through the living room, Dell up and follows.

Through the window, Janna sees Sheriff Trucks, Vet Vans and
horse trailers pulling up.

> JANNA
> (beat)
> They're coming to take our horses!

EXT. CONNELLY RANCH, HOUSE - MORNING - DAY

Armed deputies with drawn rifles fan about the property.

Sheriff Bostwick, Deputy Carl, Victoria Morel approach the
house.

In the background, Vet Techs and workers emerge from the line
of horse trailers extending down the road.

Janna and Dell meet Sheriff Bostwick, Carl and Victoria at
the edge of the porch.

                    SHERIFF BOSTWICK
          We've heard you're readying a sale
          of some horses. Just need to make
          sure they're clean animals - spot
          inspection according to the State
          Attorney's directives.

Dell peruses the Sheriff's horse trailers.

                    DELL
          Looks like you already made up your
          mind, Roger.

A HONKING HORN screams its way up the Connelly road.

Marla's car slides to a halt and she gets out. The armed
deputies half-point their weapons at her.

Marla gives them a look to back-off.

                    MARLA
          I'm a licenced vet here to
          corroborate any action that may be
          taken. I'll be looking at your
          paperwork, Dr. Morel.

EXT. CONNELLY RANCH - MORNING - DAY

The Vet Techs and workers head-off into the barn, fields and
corrals - others ready the horse trailers.

Victoria hands over a seizure order to Dell.

                    DELL
          Where you taking 'em.

                    VICTORIA MOREL
          They'll be well-cared for..

Chaos. Horse trailers and workers move horses separating them
for loading.

Janna arrives along with Marla.

                    JANNA
          Let me see that.

Janna hands the order to Marla. Marla quickly scans the
paperwork.

                    MARLA
          They can't take these horses with
          this seizure order.
                    (MORE)

                    MARLA (CONT'D)
          It's incomplete. This is bullshit,
          Victoria.

                    VICTORIA MOREL
          I'm the county vet with the
          authority.

Janna takes out her phone and snaps a few photos - sending
them to Vin.

                    SHERIFF BOSTWICK
          Well, you're going to need a judge
          to tell me otherwise.

INT. PAXTON, COURTHOUSE - MORNING

Vin, his phone pings - photos received. He spots a JUDGE
WILLIAMS (60'S) ahead of him in the hall.

                    VIN
          Judge Williams! Beautiful morning
          isn't it? Lemme bend your ear a
          tick.

EXT. CONNELLY RANCH - MORNING

Janna hurries up to a knot of workers struggling with a
horse. The horse's lead rope is tangled.

                    JANNA
          Hey! Hey! You can't do it like
          that! You'll hurt him.

Janna gets between the horse and the workers and unloosens
the lead rope. Then she hands it back.

                    JANNA (CONT'D)
          There? See?

She crosses over to Hudson.

Behind her, the Vet Tech pulls on the rope. The knot slips
open. The horse trots back into the field with the workers
pursuing.

INT. PAXTON, COURTHOUSE - MORNING

Vin leaves Judge Williams office.

                    VIN
          Uff da!

Regrouping, he knocks on the next door available - JUDGE
BAXTOR.

EXT. CONNELLY RANCH - DAY

Vet Techs load horses on the ramp. Sabotaged, the ramp
collapses sending a worker tumbling.

INT. PAXTON, COURTHOUSE, BATHROOM - MORNING

JUDGE VALLECAS (60'S) emerges from the toilet stall to wash
his hands. Vin hands him a towel.

                    VIN
          Hello, Judge. Got a minute?

EXT. CONNELLY RANCH, FIELD - DAY

Janna crosses the yard and heads directly toward Deputy Carl
Haggen.

                    JANNA
          Carl? CARL??

The Deputy turns.

                    DEPUTY HAGGAN
          Yes, Ma'am?

                    JANNA
          Is this how you become a man, Carl?
          Pushing local ranchers around,
          people you've grown up with your
          whole life?! That's not the
          preacher's son I used to know.

INT. PAXTON, COURTHOUSE, JUDGE'S OFFICE - DAY

Judge Vellecas' eyes the injunction.

                    VIN
          We read the seizure order is
          illegal, your honor. Animal
          examination records are incomplete.

EXT. CONNELLY RANCH - DAY

Phone in one hand, Janna stands on the ramp of a horse
trailer, blocking the Workers from loading a horse.

Dell, Marla and Hudson flank her.

The Sheriff, Morel and Carl approach.

                    SHERIFF BOSTWICK
          You need to move off that trailer,
          Ms. Connelly.
                    (MORE)

                    SHERIFF BOSTWICK (CONT'D)
          You may be violating the Federal
          Horse Protection Act which means
          federal time if indicted.

                    JANNA
          A Court Order based on old
          information? Not too valid,
          Sheriff. I handed Marla's findings
          in at the court house myself with
          my attorney.

                    SHERIFF BOSTWICK
          I could arrest you right now for
          obstruction of justice. How are you
          going to help your father from
          jail?

                    JANNA
          No matter what's the truth, huh?

                    SHERIFF BOSTWICK
          If she doesn't move, arrest her,
          Carl. If she resists, that's on
          her.
               (to the workers)
          Load 'em up!

Janna's phone BUZZES. She looks, then grins at the Sheriff.

                    JANNA
          You're going to want to answer
          that.

                    SHERIFF BOSTWICK
          Answer what?

His PHONE RINGS.

                    JANNA
          That's your judge. You're not
          taking our horses.

INT. CONNELLY RANCH, HOUSE - LATER - NIGHT

Janna, Hudson, Dell, Vin and Marla gather around the table
meal.

                    VIN
          Once Judge Vallecas saw that Dr.
          Marla's assessment was missing from
          the Seizure Order, he gave us a
          preliminary injunction.
               (MORE)

                         VIN (CONT'D)
              Everything is held in place -
              horses, criminal charges, and so
              forth - until we appear in court.
              Course, if they find new evidence
              they can act on it, but for now we
              have some breathing room.

                         JANNA
              We handed that paperwork to the
              clerk ourselves. There's no way it
              just went "missing".

Dell shakes his head.

                         DELL
              Every time we pull our heads up,
              they just push us back under.

                         VIN
              I can dig through the public county
              records. See if they let something
              slide between crossing their "t's"
              and dotting their "i's"

                         MARLA
              Let me talk to some of the other
              vets in other counties. I'm sure
              someone like Victoria Morel has a
              few skeletons in her closet.

                         JANNA
              I just keep thinking about Old Man
              Rafferty. The same thing happened
              to him, but no one seems to know
              where his horses went.

                         DELL
              Maybe that reporter knows?

                         JANNA
              The reporter from the Gazette?

                         DELL
              No, young guy from Fergus Falls
              Daily. He was out interviewing
              ranchers, writing a Sunday piece.
              He was the one who wrote that
              article on Hoag.

INT. FERGUS FALLS MINNESOTA - THE DAILEY OFFICE - DAY

Janna sits across from reporter, Josh Falvey. The RAFFERTY
RANCH ARTICLE is on the table.

                    JOSH
          Your Dell Connelly's daughter?

                    JANNA
          That's right.

                    JOSH
          I read the hit-job the Gazette did
          on your father.

                    JANNA
          To say the least.

                    JOSH
          Well, I appreciate you coming up to
          Fergus Falls this morning. Long
          drive. What can I do for ya'?

                    JANNA
          I'd like to talk to you about the
          article you wrote on Hoag Rafferty.

                    JOSH
          The rancher.

                    JANNA
          Yes. I'm curious, you never say
          what happened to his horses.

                    JOSH
          After the coroners office was done,
          they were hauled off on trailers
          somewhere.

                    JANNA
          Why'd you pick the Rafferty ranch?

                    JOSH
          You seem to be driving at
          something?

                    JANNA
          I noticed you didn't get a quote
          from the coroner's office, you just
          referred to the coroner's report.
          No quote from Sheriff Bostwick who
          was there either?

                    JOSH
          And?

                    JANNA
          Kind of a light article for these
          parts isn't it?
                    (MORE)

                    JANNA (CONT'D)
              A dead man in a barn and the
              seizure of his property?

The color in the reporter's face begins to change.

                    JANNA (CONT'D)
                    (realizing)
              You're scared of something?

                    JOSH
              You weren't there.

                    JANNA
              But, you were. And, you saw
              something, and your article didn't
              account for it. Please.

Josh hesitates, finally gets up and locks the door.

                    JOSH
              Ah, fuck me...

The reporter falls quiet, he opens up a drawer, pulls out a
file.

                    JOSH (CONT'D)
              It wasn't just a suicide.

INT. 1997 CHEVY SUV - 7:30 AM - DAY (FLASHBACK)

The reporter ambles up the rural road in his outdated, dirty
SUV.

Josh sips his coffee. KWGO Minot Radio spills with weather
reports and news.

                    JOSH (V.O.)
              I'd gotten an anonymous tip about
              Hoag Rafferty neglecting his herd.

From Falvey's POV, Dell and Gardner unload feed from their
truck.

                    JOSH (V.O.)
              The other ranchers were feeding the
              thin animals. Your father, Mr.
              Gardner.

EXT. HOAG RAFFERTY FIELD GATE - 7:35 - DAY (FLASHBACK)

Josh's SUV comes a stop near Dell and Tom.

He gets out of his vehicle - approaches Dell and Tom with a
coffee-stained shirt and crotch.

                    JOSH
          Morning, boys. Josh Falvey from the
          Fergus Falls Daily.

                    TOM
          Looks like some coffee had you for
          breakfast.

INT. FERGUS FALLS MINNESOTA - THE DAILEY OFFICE - DAY

Josh places a series of pictures forward of horses in Hoag's
field.

                    JOSH
          They weren't neglected. A little
          skinny from the winter - but
          everyone's were.

EXT. RAFTERY RANCH, BARN - DAY (FLASHBACK)

Sheriff's patrol car sits parked before the barn.

                    JOSH (V.O.)
          Your pa said Rafferty was in the
          barn, so I walked over.

EXT. HOAG RAFFERTY BARN - EARLY MORNING - DAY (FLASHBACK)

Josh, circles the Sheriff's patrol vehicle and walks toward
the opening of the barn door.

                    JOSH (V.O.)
          I looked back to see your father in
          the field, Mr. Gardner still at the
          truck getting the hay out. I didn't
          think much of it. I took a few
          pictures of the ranch, wanted to
          get a quote from Mr. Rafferty -
          every day stuff, really.

INT. FERGUS FALLS MINNESOTA - THE DAILEY OFFICE - DAY

Janna, still.

                    JANNA
          Then what happened?

                    JOSH
               (beat)
          I went inside the barn.

EXT. RAFFERTY BARN - EARLY MORNING - DAY (FLASHBACK)

Josh enters from a small access door and steps inside.

                    JOSH (V.O.)
          I saw the rancher and the Sheriff
          at the end of the stalls on the
          inside. The old man was pleading
          with him. It felt like I was
          intruding, so I just stepped behind
          a feed stack - would stay out of
          the cold, get a quote after they
          were done.

Old Man Rafferty implores his case with the Sheriff.

INT. RAFTERY RANCH, BARN - DAY (FLASHBACK)

Josh positions himself up on the stacks to get a good visual
of the exchange. The Sheriff moves closer to Hoag.

                    JOSH (V.O.)
          Then he began to work on him. Work
          on him real hard. It was more than
          the horse the Sheriff was after.

                    SHERIFF BOSTWICK
          There's nothing to be ashamed about
          it Hoag. All the stress, all the
          cold. Being alone way out here in
          Cottonwood on your own. Wife gone,
          family gone. Sick animals.
          Impossible amount of work to do.

The Old Man casts his eyes down.

                    OLD MAN RAFFERTY
          ...everything I've worked for.

                    SHERIFF BOSTWICK
          None of that is forgotten.

Sheriff Bostwick crosses over and hands the Old Man his gun.

                    JOSH (V.O.)
          Then he gave him his service
          revolver.

The Sheriff stands back.

                    SHERIFF BOSTWICK
          Safety's to the right beneath the
          trigger guard.

Hoag looks at the weapon then back at the horse.

                    SHERIFF BOSTWICK (CONT'D)
          Sometimes it sticks. Just push it
          free.

Josh moves closer to see the downing of Hoag's horse.

                    JOSH (V.O.)
          I thought he was going to take out
          the mare in the stall.

                    SHERIFF BOSTWICK
               (beat)
          All of this suffering will be over,
          Hoag.

Hoag, without thinking about it, places the gun to his head,
and pulls the trigger. POW!!

INT. FERGUS FALLS MINNESOTA - THE DAILEY OFFICE - DAY

Josh and Janna quietly sit after the recounting.

                    JANNA
          That's murder.

                    JOSH
          An argument could be made.

                    JANNA
          You were in the barn.

                    JOSH
          I stepped out before the Sheriff
          could piece together that I may
          have seen the whole thing. I heard
          Tom Gardner yell,

EXT. RAFFERTY RANCH, FIELD - DAY (FLASHBACK)

Josh runs from the barn.

                    JOSH (V.O.)
          I just ran to where your father
          collapsed.

INT. FERGUS FALLS MINNESOTA - THE DAILEY OFFICE - DAY

Quiet. Josh, a bit relieved his truth is shared.

                    JANNA
          Didn't want to go to the
          authorities?

                    JOSH
          I checked his record, career.
          Decorated military service. His
          word against mine. No one else to
          corroborate. The gun was in the
          man's hands. The Sheriff said he
          was helping him put a horse down -
          caught him off guard. Pick one.

                    JANNA
          And, the horses?

EXT. RAFFERTY RANCH - DAY (FLASHBACK)

Josh stands by taking photos. A number of HORSE TRAILERS pull
away from Rafferty's ranch.

                    JOSH(V.O.)
          This lady, Dr. Morel. She shows up,
          begins collecting horses.
          Separating them out on different
          trailers. Claimed animal abuse.
          Title 38.

INT. FERGUS FALLS MINNESOTA - THE DAILEY OFFICE - DAY

Josh hands the entire folder over to Janna.

                    JOSH
          Here.

She opens it up, revealing a number of Rafftery's personal
papers, livestock photos, and county property records.

                    JOSH (CONT'D)
          This is the stuff I came across
          while building a file after he
          died. I was afraid to do anything
          with it.

Inside the livestock photos, there's a familiar face next to
a dun mare - it's Brock McCarty.

                    JANNA
          This guy, here. Was his name Brock
          McCarty?

                    JOSH
          That doesn't ring a bell. Let me
          check my notes real quick.

He thumbs through a yellow pad, page over page.

                    JOSH (CONT'D)
          A guy named, Sam Mansfield.

                    JANNA
          And he worked for Rafferty?

                    JOSH
          He did. But he quit by the time I
          had gotten out there.

Josh hands Janna his card.

                    JOSH (CONT'D)
          If I can be of anymore help to you,
          let me know.

INT. CONNELLY RANCH, HOUSE - NIGHT

Team Connelly, Janna, Vin, Dell, Marla and Hudson gather
together over files, boxes and papers.

                    VIN
          Mansfield, Mansfield. They had to
          submit Dr. Morel's bona-fides to
          the Court as part of her
          assessment.

Vin digs through the files and pulls out a paper, reading
quickly.

                    VIN (CONT'D)
          Here it is. Morel lists a "Sam
          Mansfield" as part of her old
          practice in Leman County. Brock is
          definitely connected to Morel.

                    MARLA
          I asked around and apparently Morel
          got in hot water in Leman County
          for an insurance scam. Have someone
          accuse someone of mistreating their
          pet then offer few expensive tests
          that'll will prove their innocence.

                    JANNA
          Brock and Morel are probably still
          working together. But we're missing
          something. Like where the Rafferty
          horses went. If we find that out,
          we might just learn what they did
          Roan.

                    HUDSON
          Anyone ever hear about a Blue
          Orchid Ranch?

                    JANNA
          Why?

                    HUDSON
          This is a bunch of paperwork the
          Sheriff Department filed before
          they got their Seizure Order. On
          this transport slip, that Deputy
          Carl fellow was suppose to take
          some of our horses to a Sarah
          Windgate at the Blue Orchid Ranch.
          There's an address.

INT. PAXTON, SHERIFF DEPARTMENT - NIGHT

Carl enters Sheriff Bostwick's empty office, and drops a file
onto the desk.

As he turns to leave, curiosity gets the better of him. He
goes back to the Sheriff's desk, opens up his top drawer and
reaches for the cabinet key.

He moves to the cabinets - places the key inside the lock,
and opens up the Sheriff's private files.

He finds, slaughterhouse photos of horses, abuse, transport
trailers, seizure orders, etc.

                    DEPUTY HAGGAN
          Goddamnit...

He shuts the cabinet - fears confirmed.

EXT. BLUE ORCHID RANCH, HILL - DAY

Janna and Hudson crawl to the top of a hill overlooking the
Blue Orchid Ranch. Hudson looks through a pair of binoculars.

                    JANNA
          What do you see?

Below, a very-well funded horse ranch. Construction crews
work on a larger barn and a other buildings.

                    HUDSON
          Looks like they're expanding.
          They've definitely separated out
          the one's they're keeping from the
          ones they're shipping.

                    JANNA
          Holding ranch?

                    HUDSON
          Or, the last stop before the
          slaughterhouse.

Hudson gives Janna the binoculars.

                    HUDSON (CONT'D)
          Take a look.

Janna scans. Below, Victoria Morel walks with the foreman
pointing to a set of plans.

                    JANNA
          Sarah Windgate looks a lot like
          Victoria Morel.

Janna hands the binoc's back to Hudson.

                    JANNA (CONT'D)
          Shit. It's a racket. Morel's
          operating as Saran Windgate to get
          these horses shipped.

                    HUDSON
          The reporter said Morel only took
          the best ones. What happened to the
          rest of them?

                    JANNA
          There's one guy we know who was
          part of transporting horses here.

INT. BULL-N-BREW SALOON - NIGHT

Deputy Carl slumps at the bar, two empty glasses in front of
him. Bartender washes glasses - Carl ponders his future.

Janna steps up next to him and sits.

                    JANNA
          Whatever he's drinking.

                    DEPUTY HAGGAN
              (drunkenly turns)
          You...

                    JANNA
          Hi, Carl. Out of uniform today. Day
          off?

                    DEPUTY HAGGAN
               (distracted)
          Yeah, day off.

                    JANNA
          I saw you sitting here. Listen, I
          just want to apologize for the
          unloading on you at the ranch. You
          gotta' job to do. I should respect
          that. Was out of line.

Bartender arrives with a drink.

                    JANNA (CONT'D)
          Can I get you another one, Carl?

Suspicious, but...

                    DEPUTY HAGGAN
          Sure. Why not?

                    JANNA
          Whatever he's having. My tab.

                    DEPUTY HAGGAN
               (sloshy)
          I suppose I'd feel the same if I
          were in your shoes. Ranchers, all
          over the valley. They're all pissed-
          off.

                    JANNA
          How many?

                    DEPUTY HAGGAN
          Rafferty wasn't the first. Far from
          it.

Drinks. Janna - observant - playing it cool.

                    DEPUTY HAGGAN (CONT'D)
          You know, it's not like I am new at
          this, right? I took the law
          enforcement course at the Community
          College. I'm ready for it. Or,
          thought I was ready.

                    JANNA
          You're a good deputy, Carl. I don't
          know how you do it, really. And,
          Victoria Morel? She tends to ride
          part in parcel with the Sheriff
          doesn't she?

                    DEPUTY HAGGAN
          She's a cold piece of work.

                    JANNA
          What do you mean?

                    DEPUTY HAGGAN
          She'd sell her mother down the road
          for a bag of chicken feed.

                    JANNA
          You think she's after Dell,
          personally?

                    DEPUTY HAGGAN
          Nah, she doesn't care for anyone
          but herself. Your old man just
          isn't worth as much as 70 horses.

                    JANNA
              (beat)
          Well, if its for the best, its for
          the best. Bet you're tired of
          driving over all the time to her
          clinic in Lynden with the paperwork
          aren't ya?

                    DEPUTY HAGGAN
              (fading)
          Sheriff's got me doing it two-three
          times a week. Her field trailer-
          clinic is way out there. Just
          getting back takes me an hour.

                    JANNA
          You work hard, Carl.

                    DEPUTY HAGGAN
              (fading)
          I could've just... done the online
          course... to be an appraiser in
          Fargo... for all the good the law
          class certificate got me.

Deputy Carl - Out! Head on the bar. Janna stuffs some napkins
under his cheek - lays down some money on the counter-top.

                    JANNA
          Make sure he gets a ride home will
          you? Goodnight, Carl

EXT. VICTORIA MOREL'S VET CLINIC - LYNDEN - NIGHT

Janna drives on a dirt access road and turns the lights off
on her car. In the distance, Victoria Morel's clinic.

She gets out of her car, quietly closes the door and makes
her way around the back of the modular trailer.

INT. VICTORIA MOREL'S VET CLINIC - LYNDEN - NIGHT

Inside, a night-time cleaning company EMPLOYEE dumps baskets
in her garbage can - pushes her garbage can in the other
office room.

Janna pulls a hoodie over her head, let's herself in - a
small pin-light leads the way to Victoria's files.

Keeping her eye on the woman in the other room, Janna's
fingers rifle through seizure slips - falsified medical
reports, horse shipments and more.

                    JANNA
                (whispering)
          Blue Orchid.

INT. CONNELLY RANCH, BUNK HOUSE - NIGHT

Janna slides inside Hudson's door. She sees Hudson who is
taking a shower. She turns her head, knocks three times on
the wall.

                    JANNA
          Matt!

Matt turns, loaded up with soap.

                    HUDSON
          Hey!

Janna throws a towel in his face - half looking, half not.

                    HUDSON (CONT'D)
          Hey! I told you about protocols! If
          you need a scratchin'! You mind?
          I'm a bit nekked, here!

                    JANNA
          I'm not here for that. Get dry!

BUNK HOUSE - MINUTES LATER

Hudson finishes getting dressed.

                    HUDSON
          What kind of trouble you get into
          now?

                    JANNA
          Morel's assessment of our horses.
          Right here! Bad ratings all around.

                    HUDSON
          Where did you get all this?

                    JANNA
          From Morel's field office. It was
          all out there. Here's another
          assessment of our horses. But this
          one is for a horse buyer in
          Colorado and it has glowing
          ratings.

                    HUDSON
          I take it a little fairy just
          didn't show up and give these to
          you?

                    JANNA
          Military training my friend.
          There's also a bill of sale for the
          rest of Rafferty's horses - the
          ones that didn't go to Morel's new
          ranch.

                    HUDSON
          Mexico.

                    JANNA
          And north to Canada. The horses
          were sold for slaughter to a
          factory and the Sheriff signed for
          the sale himself!

Red squad car lights then bounce about the bunk house and
barn.

                    HUDSON
          Looks like they want to have a
          talk.

Janna shoves all the paperwork under Hudson's bunk bed.

EXT. CONNELLY RANCH, HOUSE - NIGHT

The Sheriff approaches the porch along with a SECOND DEPUTY.
Dell opens the door.

                    DELL
          What is this, Les?

Janna crosses the yard from the bunk house.

                    JANNA
          Okay, okay, Sheriff. There won't be
          any trouble.

Janna arrives. With handcuffs in hand, Sheriff Bostwick
pushes past her toward Dell.

                    SHERIFF BOSTWICK
          Good.
               (looks past her)
          Dell Connelly, you are under arrest
          for multiple felony counts of
          animal abuse and neglect.

                    JANNA
          What!?!

The Sheriff steps into Dell's face.

                    SHERIFF BOSTWICK
          I'm sorry, Dell. Turn around.

Dell turns. The Sheriff places on the cuffs.

                    SHERIFF BOSTWICK (CONT'D)
          You have the right to remain
          silent. Anything you say can and
          will be used against you...

He pulls Dell past Janna.

                    JANNA
          Dell!

Dell is guided down the steps to the waiting Sheriff patrol
vehicle.

                    SHERIFF BOSTWICK
          Anything you say can and will be
          used against you in a court of law.
          You have the right to speak to an
          attorney.

Steiner and another DEPUTY puts Dell into the patrol vehicle.

INT. PAXTON, SHERIFF DEPARTMENT - FOLLOWING - DAY

Carrying the Sheriff's water, Deputy Carl walks in the
Sheriff's office with a couple cups of coffee.

Ashton Russel sits on the other side of the desk.

                    RUSSEL ASHTON
          The State Attorney General's office
          is preparing the affidavit now.

Carl hands Russel a coffee.

                    RUSSEL ASHTON (CONT'D)
          Thank you.

                    SHERIFF BOSTWICK
          If the old man goes for it.

Carl then places the Sheriff's coffee on the edge of the
Sheriff's desk - steps back, the dutiful deputy..

                    SHERIFF BOSTWICK (CONT'D)
          This will be the model moving
          forward - now that we have the
          support?

                    RUSSEL ASHTON
          Right.

Carl lingers in the room, wanting to be where the decisions
are made.

                    SHERIFF BOSTWICK
          Thanks, Carl. Shut the door on the
          way out will you?

                    DEPUTY HAGGAN
          You don't need anything else?

                    SHERIFF BOSTWICK
          Just the door, Carl. Thanks.

The men wait until Carl is out of the room.

                    RUSSEL ASHTON
          So, anyway, it should all go
          smoothly if Mr. Connelly wants to
          hold on to his property.

EXT. PAXTON, COURTHOUSE - DAY

Janna and Hudson hurry up the steps of the courthouse to
where Vin waits for them.

                    JANNA
          How's Dell? He alright?

                    VIN
          Little tired. Little shaken. Bail's
          been set. He'll walk today. They
          want to talk a deal.

                    JANNA
          Look at these.

Janna opens up her shoulder bag - shows Vin the documents
taken from the Morel clinic.

                    JANNA (CONT'D)
          Seizure orders, livestock
          assessments. Shipping documents.
          Signatures. It's all here. They're
          giving these horses new paperwork,
          washing their titles, and either
          selling them, or shipping 'em off
          to the slaughterhouses. I'm sure
          the good Sheriff is getting a nice
          cut.

Vin reviews.

                    VIN
          Where'd you get these?

                    JANNA
          Absconded? Is that the legal term?

                    VIN
          Completely inadmissible.

                    JANNA
          But at least we know the truth,
          Vin. And, that's a good place to
          start.

INT. PAXTON, COURTHOUSE, OFFICE - DAY

Janna, Hudson, Dell and Vin sit on one side of a table.

Sheriff Bostwick, Russel Ashton, sit on the other. Deputy
Carl leans against the wall nearby.

                    VIN
          Excuse me, but where's the State's
          representative?

                    RUSSEL ASHTON
          I'm Russel Ashton, United Animal
          Protection Agency. We've been given
          authority to act in the State's
          interest today.

                    VIN
And what is it you do?

                    RUSSEL ASHTON
We provide oversight to local law
enforcement in cases like these.

                    VIN
Ain't that grand. Well, its your
dime. Let's hear it.

                    RUSSEL ASHTON
We're not heartless, Mr. Connelly.
We know this has put great
emotional and financial strain on
you and the ranch. A settlement can
end all this right now.

                    VIN
You're offering a deal?

                    RUSSEL ASHTON
The state will drop the felony
criminal charges if Mr. Connelly
accepts a lesser charge.

                    VIN
And what would that be?

                    RUSSEL ASHTON
Class A dropped to Class C
misdemeanor. Animal endangerment.

                    SHERIFF BOSTWICK
It's going to mean the forfeiture
of your animals, Dell. Any future
livestock, would be limited to five
or less.

Dell sways in his chair.

                    DELL
You want me to stop ranching?
That's what you're asking?

                    RUSSEL ASHTON
It's a generous deal for someone
facing felony charges.

INT. VICTORIA MOREL'S VET CLINIC - LYNDEN - DAY

Victoria, with papers in hand, makes her way to the filing
cabinet.

She opens the drawer, revealing a missing section of files.

Shocked, she turns, looking up to the security camera mounted on the ceiling.

INT. PAXTON, COURTHOUSE, OFFICE - DAY

Janna continues.

                    JANNA (CON'T)
               (beat)
          So, this is it. This how you do it.
          To date you haven't told us where
          you've taken our horses or the
          horses of the other ranchers. We've
          asked. We have a right to know, and
          you've done nothing but stonewall.
          I came home because my father was
          sick and found the town I grew up
          in, even sicker. Found good men,
          and long-time friends, now turning
          on each other out fear - the fear
          you've caused. This land, to make
          something out of it, is hard enough
          Mr. Ashton. I take it, you probably
          don't know anything about it. But
          then you come along with all your
          "Title 38's" you can write and
          stuff in your briefcase, then set
          out to destroy a way of life, a
          tradition, and more importantly,
          the families that have been here
          for generations. So, here's what's
          going to happen. We're going to
          pass on your generous offer. Bail's
          been set, and Dell is going to walk
          out of here - right now.

Janna gets up.

                    VIN
          Gentlemen? It sounds like we'll be
          seeing you in court doesn't it?

INT. VICTORIA MOREL'S VET CLINIC - LYNDEN - DAY

Victoria sits looking at the security video.

We see a female figure, face covered, wearing a dark sweatshirt and hoodie, working through the files with a pin light.

EXT. COUTHOUSE STEPS - DAY

Janna, Dell, Vin and Hudson exit the courthouse.

                    VIN
          Harper Lee couldn't have said it
          better herself.

                    JANNA
          I'm still shaking.

                    DELL
          What now?

                    JANNA
          We know what the truth is. We just
          have to go and find more of it.

                    VIN
          Legally.

EXT. VICTORIA MOREL'S VET CLINIC - LYNDEN - DAY

Victoria paces out of earshot from anybody.

                    VICTORIA MOREL (PHONE)
          Sheriff. You better pull something
          out of your ass, because if you
          don't, we're all going down!

INT. SHERIFF PATROL VEHICLE - DAY

The Sheriff and Russel Ashton sit in Steiner's patrol car.
The Sheriff puts down his phone.

                    SHERIFF BOSTWICK
          They're were some files taken out
          of Victoria's field office. Like
          someone knew where to look.

                    RUSSEL ASHTON
          The girl?

                    SHERIFF BOSTWICK
          Probably.

                    RUSSEL ASHTON
          Maybe she just needs to be sent a
          message, regardless.

The Sheriff reaches for his cell phone.

                    SHERIFF BOSTWICK (PHONE)
          Brock. Wake up. Time to go to work.

EXT. CONNELLY RANCH ROAD - DAY

Janna's car pulls out from the service road. She makes a left
hand turn.

Brock sits in his bondo-covered Jeep, Pick-Up truck.

EXT. RAFFERTY RANCH - DAY

Janna pulls her car into the front of Old Man Rafferty's
house. The ranch house is boarded up - desolate - not an
animal in the field - an old man's life and work, now an
apparent wasteland.

Janna approaches the barn.

INT. RAFTERY RANCH, BARN - DAY

Janna steps in. Long, thin streams of light penetrate the
barn's ship-lap siding and lays streams of light along the
barn's floor.

She carefully walks the barn - looking down as she walks,
looking for any kind of piece of evidence - anything at all.

She looks up and inventories the roof ceiling - nothing out
of the ordinary. The sound of a light-wind whistles through
the rafters.

INT. DEPUTY CARL'S PATROL CAR - DAY

Deputy Carl is parked on the side of the road - paperwork. A
call comes in.

                    RADIO
          Carl, we got a call, possible 5924
          out at the abandoned Rafferty
          ranch.

                    DEPUTY HAGGAN
          What's that again?

                    RADIO
          Trespassing, Carl.

INT. RAFFERTY RANCH - DAY

Janna stands where the Sheriff would have stood, then steps
to where Hoag Rafferty would have stood.

She holds out her hand like she's holding a weapon. She
follows the line of the shot, crosses and sees the shattered
window.

Janna then turns and approaches a horse stall. She opens it, and steps inside.

Inside the stall, she pushes the hay around with her feet. The front part of her boot, rolls up and over a small object beneath the hay.

Janna bends down. She pushes away the hay exposing the floor of the stall. She looks to see a dark glass vile.

It reads: Potomac Virus - Extreme Danger. She puts it in her pocket.

She then looks up to see Brock swinging down onto her a hurling, six-foot rusty shovel.

                    JANNA
          No!

Janna turns away from the swing - the shovel digs into the barn floor next to her. Mud and hay fly!

She dives and tumbles into the stall next to her. Janna looks for a weapon but none to be had.

Brock leaps up the stall- and takes a vicious, slicing second swing toward Janna's head, digging into stall boards near Janna's face.

Crash! Wood chips fly! Brock quickly circles but Janna pushes open the second stall smacking into Brock and driving him back down.

Janna bolts toward the open barn. Brock gets up and gives chase.

Brock cover and gains ground on her. She runs to a wooden wall ladder - rapidly climbs up its rungs - Brock presses wildly swinging his shovel just hitting below her feet.

Whack! Whack! Janna kicks and claws!

Janna jumps over Brock landing hard on the barn floor and tumbles. He rushes her again.

Janna gets up and begins sprinting to the far side of the barn on a flat out run. Brock makes up ground by throwing a two foot 2 x 4 squarely in her back.

                    JANNA (CONT'D)
          Arrhhh!!

She flies slamming face first into a standing barn beam. Her phone drops from her pocket.

                         JANNA (CONT'D)
          Arrgghh!

Brock approaches and grabs her phone.

                         BROCK
          Nothing like swinging for the
          fences!

He tosses it like a softball pitch and swings away. The phone
- 100 pieces.

                         BROCK (CONT'D)
          What do you think? Out of the park?

He then turns and wields the shovel in swinging motions
toward Janna. But she rushes him rather than running.

Brock squares up a barrage of hand to hand fighting. Janna's
training holds up under fire. A right, a counter, a drop whip
to the legs - Brock goes down.

Janna gets up and sprints for Hoag's old work bench loaded
with old rusty tools - now weapons.

Frantically, she finds an old staple gun - Brock slams into
her from behind - she turns and squeezes the staple gun into
his face, a hard tack staple in Brock's eye.

Brock stumbles backward.

Janna spins back to the bench, looking for more weapons.

Brock picks himself up and launches a hard, driving kick into
her from behind - pushing Janna hard up against Hoag's work-
bench.

                         JANNA
          Ahh!

Her hands scramble - she finds a rusty hammer - grips it.

Brock grabs her from behind, and begins to choke her. Janna
struggles trying to breathe. She then steps on his foot hard,
turns, whips and head-butts her forehead into Brock's face.

                         BROCK
          You fucking bitch!!

Brock staggers backwards. Janna sprints for the open barn
door.

Brock gets up, grabs the nearby shovel, cocks his hips and whirls it towards the fleeing Janna, smashing her back and legs driving her down once again.

Brock then rushes Janna to finish her off.

Janna turns from her stomach, onto her back, to see Brock running directly at her - coming hard.

From the floor, she finds the hammer - Janna wields the mallet overhead, launching it, letting it fly!!

Hoag's rusty hammer cuts through the air, end-over-lethal-end and greets the rushing Brock McCarty square in the forehead.

                    BROCK (CONT'D)
          Arrgghhh...

He drops like a led zeppelin from the sky where Hoag Rafferty met his end.

Brock's flip phone rings. Janna reaches for it, flips it open. She takes a breath. She says nothing.

INT. BOSTWICK'S GARAGE - DUSK

Bostwick cleans the heads of his golf clubs.

                    SHERIFF BOSTWICK
          Is it over?

INT. RAFFERTY RANCH - DAY

Janna steps away from Brock's body.

                    JANNA
          We're just getting started, Roger.

Janna closes the phone. She stands, reaches in her pocket for Josh Falvey's business card - dials again and on the other line - Josh Falvey.

                    JOSH FALVEY (V.O.)
          Ferguson Dailey. Josh Falvey.

                    JANNA
          Janna Connelly, Josh. Get out to
          the Connelly Ranch. If I'm right, I
          think you'll find me in the barn.
          The end of your story is about to
          be written.

Janna begins toward the barn opening, dialing the ranch.

Brock's phone just dies in her hands - no screen light, no power.

                    JANNA (CONT'D)
          Great...

EXT. RAFTERY RANCH, BARN - DUSK

Janna, deeply bruised, full sprint, runs to her car.

EXT. RAFFERTY RANCH ACCESS ROAD - DUSK

Janna makes a hard right, and guns for home.

EXT. RURAL ROAD - RAFFERTY ROAD - DUSK

Carl sees an old, bondo'd Pick-Up Truck. He makes the turn up the road.

EXT. OPEN ROAD - DUSK

Sheriff Bostwick's patrol vehicle flies flat out at high-speeds toward the Connelly ranch.

EXT. VICTORIA MOREL'S VET CLINIC - LYNDEN - NIGHT

Carrying incriminating boxes out of her of office, Victoria Morel loads up her car under the cover of darkness.

EXT. RAFTERY RANCH, BARN - NIGHT

Deputy Haggen checks out the parked jeep - nothing there.

INT. RAFTERY RANCH, BARN - DUSK

He opens the barn door. His flashlight crisscrosses the dark floor throughout.

He then comes across the dead body of Brock McCarty. He approaches - examines the fatal defensive wound and the rusty hammer which lies nearby.

                    DEPUTY HAGGAN
          Shit.

EXT. RURAL ROAD - DEPUTY'S PATROL CAR - NIGHT

Traveling at 100 MPH plus - the Deputy races to the Connelly Ranch.

EXT. CONNELLY RANCH, HOUSE (VARIOUS) - NIGHT

With her headlights turned off, Janna eases up to the barn without notice.

Parked behind the barn out of sight, the Sheriff's patrol vehicle.

She gets out of the car and makes for the barn.

INT. CONNELLY RANCH, BARN - NIGHT

Janna enters the barn - alone. Dark, sparse pools of light.

Sheriff Bostwick stands in the middle of the barn - waiting.

                    JANNA
          I had a feeling you'd show up in my
          barn again.

                    SHERIFF BOSTWICK
          Looks like you gave Brock all he
          could take?

                    JANNA
          Looks like.

Janna tosses out the Potomac virus vial. It lands between them.

                    JANNA (CONT'D)
          Potomac Fever, huh? Clever. Hired
          help lays the groundwork so the
          horses get sick, Victoria Morel
          confirms it, your hands are tied,
          nothing else you can do but take
          the livestock.

                    SHERIFF BOSTWICK
          Smart girl.

                    JANNA
          And, Hoag Rafferty?

                    SHERIFF BOSTWICK
          Shame what happened.

Reporter Josh Falvey enters the rear of the barn and stands hidden near a haystack.

He records the conversation with his phone.

                    JANNA
          Bet it was - but, talking him into
          it. That's whole different story
          isn't it?

                    SHERIFF BOSTWICK
          What do you mean by that?

> JANNA
> He actually did your dirty work for
> you. You have the perfect alibi.
> You witnessed his suicide. Horse
> was sick, too much work on the
> ranch. You hand him over your
> service revolver. Doing him a
> favor, right Sheriff?

> SHERIFF BOSTWICK
> The old man's time had come.

> JANNA
> Did it? Was it his time? Or, did
> you help him along with it? Old
> man, vulnerable. He pulls the
> trigger on himself. A jury just
> might call that being an "accessory
> to murder", Sheriff.

> SHERIFF BOSTWICK
> Those are big boy words, Miss
> Connelly. I came out hoping you
> listen to reason - take the plea
> deal. But it looks like we're a
> little beyond that now, aren't we?

> JANNA
> You going to kill me? You going to
> kill all the ranchers who get in
> your way? Dell? Was it your plan to
> talk him into pulling the trigger
> on himself at some point?

> SHERIFF BOSTWICK
> Making this look like self-defense
> is a pain and more paperwork for
> me, but if that's how you want to
> play it.

CLICK. The sound of a gun being cocked.

Deputy Carl Haggen steps into view, pointing his gun vaguely
toward the Sheriff but not directly at him.

> DEPUTY HAGGAN
> Don't do this, boss. Please. Put
> down the gun.

> SHERIFF BOSTWICK
> Get out of here, Carl. You're in
> over your head. Just walk away.

> DEPUTY HAGGAN
> I can't do that. I've looked the
> other way for a long time. I can't
> do it anymore. Not when it comes to
> this.

> SHERIFF BOSTWICK
> You'll do what I say, Deputy! I'm
> the sheriff!

> DEPUTY HAGGAN
> No... I won't be doing what you
> say. You're under arrest.

> SHERIFF BOSTWICK
> Ah, you disappoint me.

The Sheriff turns suddenly toward Carl, gun coming into line.
BA-BANG! The two guns go off simultaneously.

Janna darts into stall but now pinned down.

INT. CONNELLY RANCH, HOUSE - NIGHT

Dell and Hudson hear shots fired from the barn. Both make for
the front door.

> DELL
> Janna!

INT. CONNELLY RANCH, BARN - NIGHT

Carl lies with a major gun wound to the chest and shoulder.
The Sheriff takes up a position hidden behind a tack wall -
he too is hit and bleeding.

Josh throws a bucket across the barn creating a diversion.
The Sheriff unloads his weapon at the distraction. Pow! Pow!
Pow!

Josh darts into the stall and shuts the stall gate.

> JOSH
> You hit?

> JANNA
> No. But the Deputy is.

Janna looks between the stall boards and sees Deputy Haggan
lying out in the middle of the barn - unconscious.

> JANNA (CONT'D)
> He's breathing but I gotta' get to
> him. He'll bleed out if I don't.

                    JOSH
          Where's the Sheriff?

                    JANNA
          Far side, behind the tack wall, I
          think. Near the feed stacks.

Josh looks around.

                    JOSH
          He doesn't know I'm in the barn.
          I'll climb over this stall and let
          this horse out. Smack him and get
          him riled. Create a diversion.
          We'll both run to the Deputy and
          pull him inside the stall.

Josh approaches the stall-wall - clings and climbs, makes his
way over.

EXT. CONNELLY RANCH, BARN - OTHER ENTRANCE - NIGHT

Hudson opens the other barn entrance. Pow! Pow! Pow! Hudson
covers Dell and pulls him away from the back entrance.

INT. CONNELLY RANCH, BARN - NIGHT

Josh opens the stall gate, leads the horse to the opening of
it, then smacks him on the ass! The horse bolts but with
nowhere to run but inside the barn.

Janna pushes open her stall door - both Josh and Janna run to
the fallen Deputy. They grab him by the shoulders and drag
him out of the line of fire back into the stall.

Josh grabs Carl's service revolver while Janna examines
Carl's wounds - applying pressure to his shoulder.

                    SHERIFF BOSTWICK
          Carl, dead!?

                    JANNA
          He needs medical attention. We
          can't do it in here, Sheriff! We
          gotta' put an end to this. None of
          this is making any sense?

EXT. CONNELLY RANCH, YARD - NIGHT

Hudson helps Dell to get back to the main house.

                    HUDSON
          Call the state police. I'm gonna'
          try something.

INT. CONNELLY RANCH, BARN - NIGHT

Sheriff Bostwick, with one arm limp, reloads.

                    SHERIFF BOSTWICK
          I agree. What do you suggest?

EXT. CONNELLY RANCH, BARN - NIGHT

Hudson arrives with his lasso rope in hand. He approaches the
door, quietly, carefully, pushing his way in.

INT. CONNELLY RANCH, BAR - NIGHT

Hudson positions to see the Sheriff with his drawn gun
looking across the barn - bleeding.

Hudson then climbs up and onto the stacks of hay above the
Sheriff. He positions himself without being scene - he
readies his lasso.

The restless horse moves up and down, from left to right
inside the barn itself. Hudson looks up to see a heavy wooden
cross-beam that's within reach.

He glides the end of rope over the beam and ties the end of
it off around a heavy, wired, hay bail.

Janna looks to sees Hudson from across the barn positioning
himself for the strike.

Hudson points below to where he's positioned signalling
Bostwick's location. He then motions for janna to throw
something across the barn.

                    SHERIFF BOSTWICK
          It'll be my word and badge against
          the charges Dell and you are now
          facing!!

                    JANNA
          What about Carl? You going to let
          him die?

                    SHERIFF BOSTWICK
          Deputy turned bad I guess.
          Unfortunate.

Janna throws out a feed bucket toward the horse. The horse
spooks, and rears - moves about in the barn.

The Sheriff fires! Pow! Pow at Janna's stall. Boards and wood
chips fly!

Hudson then snaps his wrist and throws the rope encircling
the Sheriff's upper torso. Hudson fiercely yanks the lasso up
and against the Sheriff's wounded arm and kicks off the
counter-weight hay bail from the stack.

                    SHERIFF BOSTWICK (CONT'D)
          Arrrrggghh!

The rope pulls, draws and tightens over the beam like a
pulley sending the Sheriff wildly swinging over the barn
floor - firing his weapon in all directions!!

Pow! Pow! Pow!!

                    SHERIFF BOSTWICK (CONT'D)
          Get me down!

Janna steps out from her stall, pointing the Deputy's
revolver at the Sheriff and takes up a position.

Bostwick swings from left to right high-above the jerking
horse.

                    JANNA
          Drop the gun!

                    SHERIFF BOSTWICK
          Cut me down!

                    JANNA
          Loose the weapon, Sheriff! Drop it.

Suddenly, the rope slips from the weight of the Sheriff's
swinging body and the lasso jimmies mercilessly up his body
and around the man's neck - tightening, choking, squeezing.

Bostwick now swings and fires wildly throughout the barn.
Pow! Pow! Pow! Buckets hit, barn tack hit, holes punched by
bullets through the barn.

The horse, with nowhere to go, dangerously rears up, steps
back, rushes forward again.

                    JOSH
          Look out!

The Sheriff strangulates ten feet above the barn floor -
spinning, kicking, fighting to get the rope free from around
his neck no can do.

Janna moves closer with Carl's drawn weapon.

>   JANNA
>   You're going to hang yourself,
>   Sheriff! If you don't drop the
>   weapon, you're going to die!

Oxygen at a minimum, the very life of the man hangs by a very secure thread. The Sheriff's hand falls limp and the gun drops beneath him.

>   JANNA (CONT'D)
>   Cut him loose, Hudson. Cut him
>   loose!

Hudson moves to the rope over the beam - he cuts the rope.

The Sheriff drops to the floor of the barn. The agitated horse shuffles forward and backward. The Sheriff works the rope from off and around his neck.

He struggles to find his gun within the mayhem of an overwrought equine.

>   JANNA (CONT'D)
>   Don't do it.

The Sheriff reaches for his gun on the floor, then looks up. The horse rears, and the Sheriff takes a point blank back kick to the head from the riled mare.

His eyes - frozen open, blood from his cracked skull covers his head and face - falls to the ground.

Our heroes circle the stall.

>   JANNA (CONT'D)
>   It's over. (beat) It's over.

INT. SHERIFF HAGGEN'S OFFICE - LATER - DAY

Carl, with a bandaged shoulder, sits behind the old desk of Sheriff Bostwick. He reads the police code manual.

A YOUNGER DEPUTY walks, now carries water for Carl, places down a coffee on his desk.

>   YOUNGER DEPUTY
>   Here's your coffee Sheriff.

INT. UAPA REGIONAL OFFICE - DAY

In a expensive looking office, Russel Ashton makes a presentation to a group of UAPA BRASS.

                    RUSSEL ASHTON
          Though we had setbacks in **North
          Dakota.**

He points toward a large MAP, other states are highlighted.

                    RUSSEL ASHTON (CONT'D)
          We have similar laws in motion,
          Montana, Idaho, Wyoming...

EXT. BLUE ORCHID RANCH - DAY

Janna and Hudson approach the equine holding area where the
horses were being held for shipment.

Roan, in the distance - still, like a horse waiting for her
time to be loaded and shipped.

                    JANNA
          There she is. Roan?

Roan turns - sees Janna - bucks and skips about making her
way from the field to swing-gate.

Hudson opens it up. The foal comes straight to Janna's
welcoming hands. She places a light lead line onto the foals
leather halter.

                    JANNA (CONT'D)
          C'mon, Roan. (beat) We're going
          home.

EXT. CONNELLY FIELD - LATER - DAY

Janna and Hudson walk the foal out to the rolling fields. The
skies are clear, the hills are spring green.

                    JANNA (CON'T)
          Okay, Mathew David Hudson. You can
          make the bunk house the way you
          want it... make you foreman, look
          after, Dell. And, when I get back,
          maybe we can...

                    HUDSON (CON'T)
          Six more months isn't that long. I
          figure a boy like me can wait for a
          girl like you.

Before them, the property's giant oak.

EXT. GIANT HILLSIDE OAK - DAY

Dell, with wheelbarrow nearby, is bent over, working the earth, planting dozens and dozens of his, flowering, Black-Eyed Susans.

Janna and Hudson approach along with the foal - Roan.

Before them, the grave of his beloved horse. Dell gets up from his knees and steps back - a quiet moment between them for the fallen, beloved fallen, family horse.

A bit of a honorarium reads on a post nearby.

                    JANNA
              (reads)
          "Here lies the one who loved us
          all, and in return, the one who was
          loved as much. And, no matter how
          deep your sleep, I will always hear
          you, old friend - and not even
          death will keep your spirit from
          running freely in my fields".

Janna steps back.

                    JANNA (CONT'D)
          Here, dad.

She hands the foal's lead line to her father. He walks the foal to the edge of the oak.

He takes a minute, thinks of his old horse, then remove's the foal's halter.

                    DELL
          There you go, girl.

Roan, unsure of herself, looks back to our heroes, then steps out from beneath the shadows of the oak.

Hesitant legs then gather in confidence.

The young horse picks up her stride - runs openly toward the green grass beneath the grave of her mother - and, freely in the fields below.

INT. FERGUS FALLS MINNESOTA - THE DAILEY OFFICE - DAY

Josh works on his computer, now writing his story. Desktop screen types out, *The Stand at Paxton County*...

We begin to fade to black...   *The End*